# Antiques & Diamonds

### Rex Merchant

Copyright © Rex Merchant Published 2015
ISBN 9781902474311

All rights reserved. No part of this book may be reproduced or
stored in an information retrieval system or transmitted by
any means, without the express permission of the Publisher
given in writing

Published by Rex Merchant @ Norman Cottage
89 West Road
Oakham
Rutland LE15 6LT

normancottage@yahoo.co.uk
www.rexmerchant.co.uk

British Library Cataloguing-in-Publication Data.
A catalogue record of this book is available from the
British Library

Typeset in Palatino Linotype 11point.
Printed and bound by
Rex Merchant @ Norman Cottage.
Cover designed by Rex Merchant

# Antiques & Diamonds

*A novel set in the world of Antiques and Drug Dealing.*

*by*

## Rex Merchant

**Published by Rex Merchant**
**@**

**Norman Cottage**

*Antique dealing and restoring is a fascinating business. There is so much to learn; one lifetime is not enough. I have had a love of antiques, especially clocks and barometers, since the 1960's and have enjoyed collecting them as well as restoring and dealing in them.*

*In all such areas of commerce, where valuable items change hands for large sums of money, there are bound to be some dishonest dealings; human nature being what it is!*

*In this fictional story where the business of antique dealing meets the murkey world of drug dealing, it is inevitable there will be danger and problems.*

Rex Merchant
Oakham
2015

## Chapter One.

"Damn these interruptions!" Christopher Doughty pushed his French-polishing rubber into a jar of methylated spirit to stop it drying and went to answer the phone.

"Hello. Barrowick Antiques. Can I help you?"

The dealer stood and listened for a few seconds before he realised who was ringing him. It was a voice from the past; an interruption, but nevertheless a welcome one. He relaxed and spoke to the caller. "Steve. It's good to hear from you again."

Steve Edmund was an old buddy. They had served together in the Parachute Regiment in Iraq during the war there. Chris greeted his old mate cheerily. "How's Cley then: still a sleepy village with no business? How's Dawn? I'm surprised she hasn't left you by now, you old reprobate."

This small talk fell on deaf ears. Steve ignored the banter and immediately explained why he had called. From his tone of voice Chris realised he was under some stress and this was not just a social call

"I've bought a longcase clock and some other antiques and I paid too much for them. Now I've got them home I realise they need quite a bit of restoration. I wonder whether you could help?"

"Is there no one else closer to you who can do the job?" Chris would like to have helped but he had plenty of work already awaiting his attention, and Cley in Norfolk was at least ninety miles from his antique business in Rutland.

"No, there's no one I can trust, or afford. I was hoping you could help me out... but if it's not convenient..." His voice tailed off, a hint of desperation in it.

"I'll make it convenient, Steve. Don't worry. I couldn't let you down."

"Thanks mate. I was hoping you would help. I'm having trouble with the bank and I must get a return on this stock as soon as possible or the business will go under."

As he listened Chris began to realise that Steve was in deep financial trouble. His antique business wasn't doing well and he had exceeded his credit from the bank. He tried to lighten the conversation by pretending to sound upset "So, you made a bad buy and you immediately thought of me? That's damn kind of you!" He joked about the situation but in reality, he knew his friend had no idea how to restore clocks. He was also aware that Steve was unable to stand and work for too long because of the bullet he took in his back; that injury had ended his army career.

Steve was silent for several seconds. When he did speak he was not in a mood for humour. "It's not like that. I just thought you could make a profit on the clock because you can

2

restore it. I'm not trying to pull a fast one on you."

Chris laughed. "I know that. Don't get upset Steve. I was just joking."

Steve returned to his problem with the grandfather clock. "I wouldn't normally bother you, Chris, but I do need the money back on this clock and it won't sell in its present state. I don't know where else to turn."

After some further questioning, Chris had a clearer idea of the situation. The grandfather clock Steve had bought, was in a green lacquered case. This was even more of a problem as lacquered furniture does not take kindly to modern centrally heated houses and is usually in a bad state. From experience, he knew bits fell off the lacquer ground as the wood expands and contracts in the warm and dry atmosphere of modern homes.

"In much of a mess is it?"

Steve went into detail. "The door lacquer is OK with only a few flakes missing from it but the base is very poor. I can hardly make out the design on it. The hinges are broken on the trunk door and the lock won't work. The glass in the arched door is broken. That's just for starters! I'm no clock man and I haven't a clue about the works."

"Sounds bad, Steve, but I really should see it first. Is the movement intact and have you got the weights and pendulum?"

"That's all here but the case is a mess. I don't know about the movement. I'm no expert on them."

"What say I drive over to Cley tomorrow and take a look at it? Will you be in? Would that be OK?"

"Would you do that? That's great. Thanks a lot Chris."

After a few minutes more of small talk, Chris rang off and considered the call. Steve had bought the clock and a few other antiques from a local man's widow. He'd paid rather too much for them and was desperate to offload them quickly. Chris knew he could restore the lacquered clock but he wasn't sure if the job would be worth taking on.

He had restored lacquer clocks before. It was a thankless and time-consuming job. Even in a good state that type of clock wasn't the most popular longcase clock with the buying public and they were a bit out of fashion for modern houses. He considered it from all angles but his overiding concern was for Steve; he was a mate and they had history. They had fought together and become very close friends when they were both in the Paras. If he could possibly help, he felt he must. What were friends for, after all? He went back to the French-polishing that Steve's call had interrupted. That conversation had given him a lot to consider, but the need to concentrate on the task in hand soon drove those concerns to the back of his mind.

The Art Nouveau cabinet being restored was already paid for and the customer was waiting to take delivery of it. It was a nice piece of furniture, veneered in Rosewood with sinuous Boxwood inlays typical of the 1890's when Art Nouveau was all the rage.

He rubbed down the first layers of French-polish that he had applied with a soft bristle brush the previous day. To avoid removing too much of it, he used a fine flour paper as an abrasive. The last coats of polish were applied with a rubber in small circular movements to build up a good layer of shellac. A final spiriting off would leave a deep satisfying shine that would enhance the grain of the Rosewood and highlight the white inlays. It was a labour of love, which he enjoyed, but it did need an experienced hand and some concentration. Concerns about Steve were put out of his mind while he worked on the cabinet.

Once the job on the cabinet was completed, he placed it in a dust free area in the corner of the workshop for the polish to harden then he went upstairs to his flat above the shop to take a break and make himself a coffee.

He stood in front of the French windows in his living room gazing out over the Rutland Water reservoir. It was a warm summer morning in Barrowick village on the South shore of the lake. The water bird; ducks, geese, waders and swans, were busy feeding along the shoreline.

His concerns for his army friend returned as soon as he relaxed and stopped working. He changed his position and glanced over the village. There was little movement on Main Street, Barrowick's only thoroughfare, which stretched from the Barrowick Arms at one end of the village to the old butcher's premises at the other end, where he had set up his antique business.

That morning the village was as quiet as a well-fed baby. The twenty stone houses with their Collyweston roof tiles, standing between the pub and the antique shop, seemed to slumber in the sunshine. Nothing stirred. His neighbours had all gone to work or driven into Oakham to shop.

A solitary car drew up in front of the church. Chris watched as John Smyth, the vicar, got out of the vehicle and walked into the church porch. The ancient church and the privately owned vicarage were the only two buildings on the opposite side of the road to the antique shop. These two substantial buildings bordered the reservoir, their golden Marlstone walls shimmering in the late morning sun.

He drained his coffee mug, the fourth that morning, and stood lost in thought. The phone call from Steve Edmunds was uppermost in his mind. It was a cry for help he couldn't ignore. Steve was an old friend. When they had served together in Iraq they had formed a firm friendship that survived even after they left the forces. He knew he must help an old comrade if he possibly could.

The unexpected phonecall that morning put the dealer in a reflective mood. He looked back on his own army career and his life since. He had joined the Paras as a teenager to escape his abusive father, who was frequently violent and had turned to drink when his wife passed away at a young age. Chris had resigned from the army soon after his father died.

With his father gone, he returned to Stamford, his home town, and soon married Vickie, a local girl. They set up an antique business in the town and were doing well until Vickie had started an affair with her ex boyfriend. Their divorce was messy. He lost the antique shop in Stamford and had to find alternative premises to start again. That was when he found the empty butcher's shop in Barrowick, a small village over the Lincolnshire border in Rutland.

When he set up his new antique shop, he knew it was not an ideal site for a retail business being a quiet backwater with no passing trade, but it was all he could afford at the time. Trade had been slow at first but his restoration skills were slowly gaining him a good reputation and he was building up a regular clientele of satisfied customers.

Soon after Chris resigned from the Paras, Steve was caught in heavy cross fire and took a bullet in his back. He was invalided out of the army and was now struggling on his pension, trying to run a small antique business on the North Norfolk coast at Cley.

Chris had a strong suspicion Steve had followed his lead into the dealing business, trying to make a living buying and selling antiques, but he knew his friend had no idea what to do with his life when his army career ended so unexpectedly. It could have been a sound business venture but Steve hadn't the restoration skills and Cley was a quiet backwater; a village that depended heavily on the seasonal holiday trade. Chris, on the other hand, had served an apprenticeship with a cabinet maker before he joined the Paras. With his skill and knowledge he could add value to any antique he bought.

The phone call from Steve had altered all the dealer's plans for the week but he had plenty of work planned for the rest of that day. He had an Edwardian bracket clock waiting to be restored. He decided to work on the clock after he'd finished the Art Nouveau cabinet.

The clock movement was sound but the case had been damaged. The veneers and beading on the front of the case had been split when someone had forceably removed a plaque from it. The clock must have been a presentation piece with a name plaque on its front but someone had prised that off and had ruined the Mahogany veneers and the Boxwood inlays in the process. It was typical of the trade buys that Chris liked to get, as he knew he could increase the value by restoring it.

Coffee break over, he returned to his workshop where

the bracket clock was awaiting his attention. He removed the movement from the clock and started to work on the wooden case. The damage was all at the front where the retaining screws had been pulled from the decorative beading at the base. He made a length of matching beading from a piece of reclaimed Cuban Mahogany. It was fine work but he was used to making such replacement pieces.

He used an antique moulding plane to make the beading to match the original pieces on the sides of the case, then sanded and stained the new piece to match. When he'd cut the beading to fit the case, he stained French polished it to match the colour of the existing wood. Once the layer of new polish was hard, he glued the replacement piece of timber to the front of the clock case.

Finally, he replaced the movement and checked the clock was working properly. The restoration took him some time so it was well into the afternoon before he felt able to leave it and consider getting some lunch.

After he'd tidied the workshop and checked on the Art Nouveau cabinet, Chris closed the shop, went up to his flat where he showered and changed out of his dusty clothes before he walked down to the Barrowick Arms hoping for a pint of beer and a sandwich. Sara, the landlady's daughter, was on duty behind the bar. She was a good friend and greeted him with a smile.

"Your usual?"

"Please. I know it's a bit late for lunch, but what sandwiches have you got left?"

"Only ham, but it is nice and lean." She looked towards the kitchen where her mother could be heard rattling pans and plates. "Mum has just taken a cooked ham joint out of the oven."

"Marvellous! Just what I need." He sat down on a barstool and picked up the local paper from the counter top.

"Not much in that this week." Sara said. "I think the local paper gets thinner by the issue."

The dealer folded the newspaper unread and replaced it on the bar. He'd had a sudden happy idea. Sara and he had a relaxed relationship; nothing too serious but they enjoyed each other's company. Perhaps she would fancy a trip to the Norfolk coast? He tentatively broached the subject with her. "It's Wednesday tomorrow. Isn't that your day off?"

Sara stopped polishing the beer glasses and looked expectantly at him. She had noticed the enthusiasm in his voice and was keen to know what he was planning.

He asked. "What about a trip to the coast?"

She put down her glass cloth and stood in front of him, her hands on her hips, an eager expression on her face. "Which coast?"

"North Norfolk. I have to go to Cley to look at a clock, but that shouldn't take me long. Fancy coming for the ride? We could make a day of it and stop off for a meal somewhere. If it's a nice day, like today has been, it will be a pleasure to escape work for a while."

Sara nodded vigorously. She had no plans for her day off and liked the idea. "I'll just have a word with mother but I can't see any problems."

"Good, I can do with the company and there's no one else I'd rather take with me."

Sara went into the kitchen. After a few minutes she

returned to the bar. "What time are we setting off?"

"Early. We can make a whole day of it. I have an appointment with an old friend who runs an antique shop in Cley next the Sea, but that shouldn't take me long The rest of the day will be ours to spend as we please."

When he returned home from the pub, Chris checked the new polish was dry on the repair he'd done to the Edwardian bracket clock then placed the clock in the centre of his shop window display, hoping to sell it quickly and make a good return on it.

The rest of the afternoon, the restorer worked on the Art Nouveau cabinet, giving it a final polish to bring the finish to perfection as it was for a regular customer who had purchased several items from him the past.

At about six o'clock, he closed the shop and went upstairs to his flat. With the day's business over, he poured himself a glass of wine and sat by the open French windows looking out over the treetops to Rutland Water. It was time to relax and think about the planned trip to Cley.

He knew Steve had his problems but there was little he could do to help him until he'd seen the clock for himself and had a chance to discuss things with him. That could wait until the morning.

The sun sank over the horizon turning the evening clouds a vivid red. The sky reflected on the surface of the reservoir turning it crimson. Chris watched the water birds drifting on the still lake, feeding before they settled down to sleep. He raised his glass and proposed a toast to a successful trip the next day then he downed the last drop of the white wine.

## Chapter Two

On the Wednesday the weather was fine. Chris picked up Sara from the pub at 7am and headed for Norfolk in his van. The roads were quiet at that early hour and they made good time. They passed through Hunstanton at about nine o'clock and were soon on the narrow coastal road heading for Cley-next-the-Sea, driving through the sleepy Norfolk villages along their way. There wasn't much traffic about that morning, giving them a chance to enjoy the scenery.

Sara noticed the flora in North Norfolk was so different from that of her home county of Rutland. The roadside verges were sandy soil so many of the wild flowers she saw were varieties only found in that dry coastal area. Occasionally they caught a glimpse of the sea out of the passenger window and they could smell the salty air. At Cley, Chris parked the van in the yard beside Steve Edmund's antique shop and pipped the horn to let him know they had arrived.

Dawn, Steve's wife, came out of the side door to greet them. "Chris, lovely to see you again." She wrapped her arms around him and gave him a hug. Stepping back she eyed Sara up and down and smiled at her, then she looked to Chris for an introduction. He could tell that from the faint smile playing on her lips and the glint in her eyes, she suspected Sara and he were an item. Married women always seemed to want to get single guys like him into long term relationships.

He introduced them. "This is Steve's wife, Dawn." Then turning to Dawn he explained "This is Sara Goodacre. She's my local barmaid and a very good friend."

Dawn grinned knowingly. "A very good friend? Don't tell me you're thinking of settling down again at last, Chris? It's about time you married again. You must be over your divorce by now. "

He could feel his cheeks colouring up and shook his head. He'd divorced his first wife, Vickie, only a few years before, and was very wary of repeating old mistakes.

Sara came to his rescue. "We are just very good friends. Chris lives in my village at Barrowick and uses our pub. It's my day off and I was at a loose end anyway."

Dawn nodded, but Chris could tell from the expression on her face that she didn't believe a word of it. She led her visitors into the house where they found her husband, Steve, sitting at the kitchen table just finishing his breakfast.

Chris chuckled. "Lucky for some. Keeping officer's hours are we? What time's this to be having breakfast?"

Steve pushed his empty plate away and got up from the table. They greeted each other like the old friends they were, slapped each other on the back and hugged.

"Sorry Chris. Didn't expect you so early. Anyway my back is playing up today. I didn't get much sleep last night.

12

I lay in bed late this morning." He winced, limped back to the table and sat heavily back in his chair. Sara and Chris sat down at the table with him while Dawn made them each a coffee.

After exchanging small talk, Chris broached the reason for his visit. "So, you've bought a lacquered longcase clock and it's in need of some TLC?"

"Aye. I didn't realise the lacquer was so damaged. I can't restore it like you can." Steve knew that Chris had served an apprenticeship in woodworking before he joined the paras and he was skilled at restoring antique furniture. He'd been over to the workshop in Barrowick a few times and had seen the work in progress there.

"We'd better take a look at this clock then." Chris stood up and pushed his chair back under the table.

In an outhouse down the yard, Steve had several antiques waiting to be cleaned and polished before he moved them into the sales area. In the far corner stood the longcase clock. Chris looked it over. It was an eight-day, brass faced, example with a silvered dial and a moving figure in the arch. He checked this automaton first. "Looks like Mercury, the messenger of the gods, by the wings on his heels and the rod he's holding."

Steve nodded.

Chris knew the figure should move from side to side as the clock pendulum swung. Clocks with automata were worth more money than standard, simple examples, so the figure mattered. The automaton did indeed move when he checked it. That was a good sign. Then he noticed that the brass dial itself was most unusual as the engraved maker's name on the cartouche it bore, was unmistakeably that of a woman. He leaned closer to check the engraving and read it aloud. "Jane Cooper. Londini. It looks genuine enough and the style of the lettering is certainly contemporary with the dial."

Steve peered closely at the silvered dial; he hadn't noticed such details.

Chris continued with his appraisal. "That's unusual, Steve. This clock was made about 1760 by the style of it. Women were not free of the Clock Company in London at that date, so her name would not normally be on there. Jane Cooper must have been the widow of a master clockmaker, that's the only way she would have been allowed to sign this clock, as it came from her late husband's workshop. It's an interesting example. Did you check in Bailey to see if she's listed?"

Steve frowned. "I hadn't got around to checking it. All I could see was the bad state of the lacquer and I know I can't restore it. I rather lost interest in it once I realised I had made a bad mistake buying it."

Chris bent down to get a closer look at the base of the clock case. "Pity that's such a mess. The door can be restored but the base is well past it. All that damaged lacquer will have to come off and a new panel prepared. I guess this clock has been stored damp, then probably kept near a central heating radiator. Lacquered wares do not take kindly to modern living. It's a mess and an expensive repair job."

Steve grimaced. He had suspected as much, but now his friend had confirmed his worst fears. It had been a big mistake buying it.

Chris removed the hood from the top of the clock and

14

checked the movement. "Eight day works and a six pillar movement. Nicely turned pillars: that's usual for quality London clocks of this period. What a pity the case is so stressed." He pressed his fingers on a motion wheel and got the clock to tick. "Doesn't look much wrong with the works that a good clean and oil won't cure." He moved the minute hand past the twelve and put pressure on the strike wheels to strike the hour. The bell was a small one and had a pleasing high-pitched ring. It had been a quality clock in its day but it was in a sorry state. He turned to face Steve and asked him the most important question. "What did you pay for it?"

"Too much I'm thinking. I gave Veronica Wilson a thousand for it."

"Phew!" Chris let out an involuntary breath. "You might get fifteen hundred for it retail, if it's fully restored, but a craftsman will charge you at least five hundred to do the work on the case."

Steve shook his head. "I thought as much, but I can't afford it. Trade's not been good."

Chris looked at the clock again and considered the work necessary. "I'll do what I can for you but maybe we can do a deal on some other things to make it worth my while taking it off your hands?"

Steve cheered up visibly at this suggestion. "Everything out here is for sale and most of it needs restoring. I know you like to buy unrestored bits so you can add value to them. Take a look. Be my guest. I hope we can come to some mutually beneficial arrangement."

Chris checked over the entire stock. Most of the bits were pot-boilers and of no use to him. Finally, he picked out

15

two items he thought he could use. "I could use that writing slope and maybe that tripod table. The writing slope needs some polishing work on the wood and some new brass inlays but I can do that. It really depends on what you want for them."

Steve checked his books. "The slope and the table came from the same lady as the clock. Her husband died suddenly quite recently. I think she's having trouble getting her hands on his money so she sold a few items off on the quiet. Me being the nearest dealer to her, she rang me and offered the bits to me."

Chris nodded. "Very local, is she?"

"Just up the road near Holt. A huge farm house set back from the road."

"What about other antiques? Any chance of buying some other items from her while I'm over here?"

"No chance. I think the estate is now all tied up legally. I understand the furniture has been removed and will all go to auction. I think the widow sold off a few items under the radar because she needed some ready cash quickly."

Chris couldn't help frowning. "Sounds a bit dodgy. Who was he, this chap that died?"

"Richard Wilson. A rich man by all accounts. He had a big house with acres of land, two jags and a racehorse in stables. He was a bit of a mystery really."

"Mystery? Why?"

"The locals can't fathom where he got his money from. They tell me he was only a booky's runner when he left school. He did a bit of inshore crab fishing and collecting Samphire on the mud flats, then suddenly he came into lots of dough.

16

He bought a sea going boat and the big house, both for cash, so they say."

"Family wealth perhaps?"

"No way. His mum still lives in a council house in Holt and she was widowed years ago. His dad used to help on the crabbing boats."

Interesting as all this conjecture was, Chris needed to get down to business, then he intended to spend the rest of the day with Sara. "Right Steve, how much for the clock, the writing slope and the table?"

"You can have them for what I paid her. That's eleven hundred and fifty in total. That way I will recoup my money and you might make something for your trouble."

It wasn't really a bargain and Chris would have normally haggled over the price to bring it down, but he didn't hesitate. He was doing an old friend a favour and he wasn't too worried about a large profit. If he could cover his costs plus a little something for the time he would have to spend restoring the clock and writing slope, he would be satisfied.

Dawn and Sara joined them in the outhouse. "Any good, Chris? Can you use the clock?"

"I think so, Dawn. I will be able to restore it and just about cover my costs."

All the time this bargaining was going on, Sara had stood quietly by the door. When it was obvious they had come to an arrangement about the items, she stepped up to her companion's side. "Can I give you a hand loading them into the van?" Chris smiled, Sara was as keen as he was to get away and enjoy their day at the coast. Once the clock and the other goods were loaded into his vehicle, he paid Steve and they said their goodbyes.

"Don't be so long calling back." Dawn scalded him. "Make sure you bring Sara with you next time. We can get to know each other better."

Back on the road, Sara started to ask a few questions. "What happened to Steve to give him that limp and a bad back?"

"Steve was involved in a fire fight with terrorists. He took a bullet near his spine when he was serving in Iraq. He was invalided out of the army and spent months in rehab."

Sara frowned. "Were you there at the time, Chris?"

"No. I'd left the paras some months before. I came out of the army just after my dad died. "

They fell silent as he drove along the coast road to Cromer where they planned to have lunch and take a walk on the pier and along the beach to relax and stretch their legs.

## Chapter Three

By lunchtime, Sara and Chris were in Cromer. It was busier there but they managed to get seated in one of the town centre restaurants and ordered their meals.

"What do you fancy?" He handed her the menu.

"Anything. It's a change not having to cook it myself."

"Well I'm having Cromer crab with a side salad. It's a local delicacy. You can't beat crab fresh and caught locally."

"Make that two then." Sara sat back and sipped her orange juice while they waited. They filled in the time with small talk. "I couldn't help hearing what you said about a lady clock maker. Is that so uncommon?"

"Very uncommon, Sara. Back in the 1700's it was men only in the clock makers' guilds. "

"So how did this one manage to get by? You said something about her being a widow."

"Yes. If her husband died and the workshop was forced to close, the apprentices and journeymen would be out of a job so the guild bent the rules and allowed the widow to carry on running her late husband's business. That's the only way she would be allowed to put her name on a London clock dial at that period."

"Does that put up the value of that clock?"

He considered that question. Sara was used to help run a pub and certainly had a good business head on her. "It may do. A serious clock collector might consider it a bonus but the average punter couldn't care less. Anyway, why this sudden interest in that clock?"

"No reason really. I was just thinking my mother put her name above the pub door as the licensee and no one bats an eyelid about that. Back in the 1700's things were very different for women." Just then the waitress arrived with their meals and put an end to all the idle conversation.

After lunch Chris drove back along the coast road, stopping off at each of the villages that bordered the sea. They passed through Sheringham and Weybourne then parked the van near the ponds at Salthouses and watched the ducks and geese, which were tame and used to being fed by the visitors. Sara, who had packed some sandwiches for herself and Chris, broke off some crusts and fed the water birds. The weather stayed fine and the sun shone all afternoon. They were both very relaxed and happy to be away from work and in each other's company for the whole day.

"We must do this more often." Chris suggested hopefully.

"I'm game. It's a pleasure to be away from the daily grind, especially in such good company." Sara checked her hair in the van mirror, well aware that he was paying her a lot of attention.

After they left Salthouses and were driving slowly through Cley, they were surprised to see both Dawn and Steve standing outside the front of their shop talking animatedly to two men. From their body language, Chris realised they were having a heated argument, so he pulled up a little way from the shop to watch what was going on. He could see the argument was getting more heated. One of the two strangers, a burly man with a bald head and a thick neck like a rugby front row forward, seemed to be losing his temper with Steve and was waving a fist at him. The other man, a tall thin chap, seemed to be asking all the questions. He kept poking his finger into Steve's chest, almost pushing him off balance. Chris decided it was getting too dangerous for his old friend. He got out of the van and went over to join him but before he left he patted Sara on her knee. "Stay where you are, Sara. This looks as if Steve's having a bit of trouble." He strode purposefully over to the group and placed himself squarely beside his mate to face the two assailants. He was just in time to catch the gist of the argument.

"You bought some antiques from Dick Wilson' wife. She told us so. We need to see them."

Steve shook his head. "I'm not denying that. But I don't have them now. I sold them on into the trade."

"Who to?" The thick set man pushed his face close to Steve in a threatening gesture then reached out to grab him by his collar.

Chris couldn't stand by and let the argument go any further. He punched the man's hand down and stepped between them.

"Who the hell are you?" The man turned on Chris,

21

glaring menacingly.

"Someone you won't want to cross." Chris waited for the man's next move, ready to react instantly. His army training took over. The man lunged at him with his fist but he was much too slow. Chris grabbed his wrist, pushed his arm high up in the air then punched him hard in his armpit. That maneuverer did the trick. His assailant crumpled onto the pavement.

Chris immediately turned on the other man. "What the hell do you think your doing, attacking people in the street?"

The man held his hands up defensively and backed away, fear showing in his eyes. He kept glancing at his companion, no doubt hoping for backup but his accomplice was still sitting on the pavement, groaning and fighting to get his breath.

"Why do you need to see these antiques?" Chris asked.

The thin man spoke up, his voice shaking with fear. "I was hoping to buy them."

"Is that how you normally buy things? With threats? Well you've come too late. You heard Steve. He said they've been sold into the trade." Turning to Steve, Chris winked at him to warn him to agree with him, then continued. "Is that the deal you were doing this morning when we called, Steve?"

Steve nodded.

Chris turned and explained. "Well, the dealers who were here were some Irish knockers, probably from Peterborough. They always park their vans at Peterborough when they come over here to buy, so you'd better go to Peterborough and try them. If you'll take my advice you won't try the heavy stuff on those boys or you'll find yourselves in the river."

"Right. It looks as if I arrived too late." The man helped his burly companion up and they walked to their car, which was parked a little distance from the shop.

Steve turned to his companion. "Thanks Chris. You arrived in the nick of time. It was getting a bit heated."

"I could see that from my van. Do you believe them? People don't usually get aggressive just because they've missed a bargain, do they?"

Steve shrugged his shoulders. "Beats me."

Sara had by this time got down from the van and joined them on the pavement. "What was that all about, Chris?"

"Nothing really. Some bloke getting irate because he'd missed a bargain."

She looked at him and raised a quizzical eyebrow. "Really? It looked more serious from where I was sitting." She wasn't convinced by his explanation and waited for a better one.

"It seems they were interested in that clock and writing slope we bought this morning, but for the life of me I can't think why"

Dawn who had stood by helpless while all this was going on, ushered them through the shop and into the kitchen where she put on the kettle for a cup of tea.

Chris checked that Steve was alright after his ordeal.

"I'm fine." Steve protested. "If they'd tried that in the old days before I took that bullet, they would have regretted it."

Chris patted him on his shoulder. "I know you can handle yourself, but two against one just wasn't fair. That's why I came over."

"Thanks mate. Just like the old times in Iraq."

23

Chris smiled. Compared to the Iraq posting that episode was like a pensioner's tea party.

"When does the rest of that Wilson woman's antiques come up for auction? Any idea? I might just come over and view if she has some good stuff like you said."

Steve stroked his chin and thought. "Dawn, pass me that auction calendar off the fridge door." He checked the dates and pointed out all the auctions that were due. "I'm certain the local auction house will handle the stuff as they have the nearest large auction rooms. I'll have to check on it and give you a ring. We could go together. At least you could advise me and stop me buying anything that needed too much work on it!"

Chris checked the dates and saw that there were two local antique and collectibles auctions listed for the next month. "Right. Give me a ring when you know the viewing dates. I will come over and meet you there, then we can both take a look. Two heads are better than one."

Sara had been listening to this conversation with growing interest. "If I can get the day off, maybe I can come as well? I've never been to an auction. I've only ever seen them on TV. It looks interesting and I'd love to go to one."

"Good. That's settled then. We'll see you in a week or two and maybe do some buying, Steve."

Dawn thanked him for stepping in to help her husband and saw them back to the van.

He apologised for rushing away. "Sorry, Dawn, but Sara and I are on our way home and she will probably be needed to help her mother get ready to run the bar in their pub this evening." That was really just an excuse, but he wanted to spend the rest of the day with Sara and they had planned to visit more of the seaside villages as they motored along the coast road towards Hunstanton. "Before we leave, I'm a bit concerned about Steve. He's not a bit like his old self. What's the score, Dawn?"

Dawn looked down at her feet. "The wound in his back is giving him a lot of trouble. Our doc thinks he may have to have another operation on his spine...and we have money problems. The business isn't doing well and I can't get any work in the area. It's just tourism and little else around here."

He patted her on the shoulder and sympathised with her. He had guessed as much when he saw Steve and the state of his shop stock. "I'll see you again when we come over to the antique sale. I'll give some thought to what can be done about the business." They said their goodbyes and left Cley.

At Holme, just before Old Hunstanton, Chris turned the van off the main road and drove along the ancient Peddar's Way through the village into the car park near the sand dunes. Sara took her bag from behind her seat and took out the remainder of the sandwiches she had brought with her.

"Very posh ham sandwiches without crusts!" She laughed as she had removed the crusts to feed the birds at Salthouse. "It's some of that ham you tried last night. I thought I'd better bring some food in case we needed it."

"Marvellous. I could just eat some of those, overlooking the sea and admiring the coastline."

They walked over the soft sand dunes and over the golf course until they found themselves on the extensive beach. To the East they could see the cliffs of the North Norfolk coast stretching towards Cromer. To the West were the sandstone cliffs of Hunstanton with the old lighthouse on top of them. The North Sea was a long way out leaving a large stretch of virgin sand, untouched and pristine.

Taking a stick from the flotsam on the high tide line, Sara ran onto the beach and drew their names in the damp sand. Chris was tempted to join her and add a heart between the names but he thought better of it. Once bitten with an unhappy relationship was once too many for him. He sat and watched her as she ran along the shoreline occasionally throwing pebbles into the sea. She was enjoying her day out. She was a smashing girl, just the sort of girl he should have married when he made the mistake of marrying Vickie.

When Sara returned to his side; he was still sitting on that grassy bank overlooking the beach and thinking about Steve's predicament. She opened the sandwiches and they ate a leisurely picnic together then both walked the sands along the edge of the sea. The sounds of the water and the cries of the Terns as they wheeled and dived into the waves for food, soon drove thoughts of Steve and his problems from his mind. To Sara's delight a seal appeared in the water just offshore from them and kept pace with them as they walked along the shoreline.

"What sort of Seal is it?" She asked.

"I'm not sure but there are colonies of Common seals and Grey seals on this coast. They are becoming much more numerous. I read somewhere we have more seals on this East coast than anywhere else in Europe."

It was a leisurely and enjoyable afternoon. By the time they returned to Barrowick it was getting dark and they were both tired but happy. Chris dropped Sara off at her home at the Barrowick Arms and parked his van in front of his premises. He unloaded the antiques he had bought from Steve, putting them in the sales area at the front of the shop until he could deal with them properly, then he took the empty van to the back yard behind the premises and walked down to his local for a drink.

## Chapter Four

Next day started with a warm summer morning in Barrowick. The sun reflected off the still surface off Rutland Water as the ducks and other water birds searched lazily for food along the water's edge. It was early and there was no movement on Main Street, the villages only thoroughfare. Chris drained his coffee mug, the third that morning as he ran on the stuff and tended to lose count of the number he drank. He stood at the French windows in his flat above the shop, gazing out at the morning, drinking in the peace and tranquility before he immersed himself in the business of the day. Suddenly his attention was brought back to reality as a police car drew up to the kerb outside his shop.

The dealer stared down as an officer got out of the car and walked briskly towards his front door. The man hammered on the door then stepped back on the pavement and looked up at window where the antique dealer was standing.

Chris raised his hand to acknowledge the policeman then put his empty coffee mug on the table. He made his way downstairs to the showroom at the front of the building and unlocked the door.

"Mr. Doughty?" The officer didn't wait for a reply but pushed past him and went to the display window, which overlooked the pavement. He pointed to the Edwardian bracket clock that stood in the front of the window. "That clock, Sir. We have reason to believe it may be stolen goods."

Chris sighed deeply. In his business, dealing in valuable antique items, there was always a risk that the stock had a doubtful history. He reached into the window, lifted out the clock and placed it on a small round oak table that stood in the sales area. "Oh dear! What can I say? I bought it in good faith."

The policeman relaxed and smiled, relieved the dealer seemed to accept the situation and was not causing a scene.

"I'll need to see your books to find where you bought it, Sir."

The dealer went into the back workshop and took his paperwork from a cupboard. "I can tell you exactly where it came from. I bought it only last month. I restored it and put it in the front of the window only a day or so ago. I'll help if I can, but tell me, why do you suspect it might be stolen?"

"An Oakham schoolboy was walking around the reservoir and spotted it in your window. He identified it immediately as a clock stolen from his grandfather's home. He rang the police station and reported it. We have a photograph of the clock on the owner's sideboard before it was taken." The policeman showed the dealer the picture. There was no doubt it was the same clock.

Chris handed back the photograph and confirmed he

could see it was undoubtedly the same clock.

The officer continued. "The boy states the clock had a brass plaque on the front of it. You can see it here on the picture. His grandfather was a railway inspector and was presented with the clock when he retired." He ran his fingers over the front of the case. "The plaque must have been removed but I can't see where it would have been."

Chris agreed again. "That's right. When I bought it there were two screw holes and some other minor damage to the front of it, but I restored it. It was obvious to me someone had forcibly removed a plaque from it. The Mahogany veneer on the front is new and so is the Boxwood inlay. I matched it up with the rest of the case."

"You understand, I shall have to take the clock, Sir. It is now an exhibit in a criminal investigation."

Chris shrugged his shoulders. This meant he would most probably lose the money he had spent buying and restoring the clock. It was a risk in his business; not one he met very often but nevertheless an unwelcome one.

"I will have to have a full description of the clock to give you a receipt, but first I need to interview you and find out how you came by it."

"OK. Look, I was just finishing breakfast when you called. Come upstairs and have a coffee while we talk."

The policeman followed the dealer up to his flat and made himself comfortable in an armchair

"Milk and sugar?" Chris called from the kitchen.

"No sugar, thanks." The man sat in the comfortable chair by the French windows and looked out over Rutland Water.

While they were drinking their coffees, the officer took

30

out his notebook and asked his questions.

Chris told him he had bought the clock in good faith from another dealer in Northamptonshire. He regularly called on several trade stops in the Finedon area. He rifled through his papers and produced the details.

The officer put down his empty mug and took out pen again. "Right, Sir. Now give me a full description of the clock so I can write you a receipt."

Chris reeled off the description. "A mahogany, inlaid, bracket clock in the Edwardian Sheraton style. It has an eight-day movement and strikes the hours on a bell. It also strikes the half hours and the quarters. It plays the Whittington Chimes. It's eighteen inches high and about ten inches wide..." He hesitated. "Anything else you need?"

The officer put his coffee mug down and read his notes. "What 's the valuation of the item?"

Chris explained. "I had it for sale at £350 and I bought it for £200."

The policeman made a note of those details then closed his notebook.

"Anything else?" Chris asked.

"No. You have been very helpful. We will follow up your information and let you know what develops. It will probably go to court and you will possibly be called as a witness."

The officer put his notebook back in his pocket and took the clock and Chris' statement with him when he left the shop.

Chris watched the squad car as it left the village. This sort of thing was bound to happen sometimes but he could lose the money and the clock; it was a good thing it didn't happen very often. He put the coffee mugs in the sink and ran them under the hot tap, then he went downstairs to his workshop to start his day.

The loss of that stock was unfortunate but he still had a lot to be thankful for. Chris had been in Rutland for three years and his antique business was slowly building up. He was gaining a reputation for restoring and selling quality antiques and the locals had begun to recommend him as a reliable dealer and restorer. It had taken time since his divorce and losing the shop in nearby Stamford, but Rutland County and Barrowick village were proving kind to him.

Later that morning, the dealer was in the workshop at the back of the premises, in the process of finishing the Art Nouveau cabinet. The inlaid cabinet was already sold but it needed some minor restoration before the customer took delivery of it. It was a warm, balmy day. The sweat stood on him as he worked. He stopped to mop the perspiration from his face and decided to remove his shirt, which was already stained with large sweat patches. He continued working in just his jeans and shoes. The polish was building into a deep satisfying shine as he worked on the wood surface so that he could see his reflection in it. He had just stopped this work and stood back to check on its progress when the shop bell sounded from the sale's area at the front of the building where the restored antiques were displayed for customers to see. He wiped his hands on an old towel and was about to put his shirt back on to go into the shop, when a young lady came through the sales area and into the back workshop.

"Oh. It only you!" He relaxed and smiles at his visitor.

32

It was Sara Goodacre who worked at the local pub, the girl had taken over to Cley to meet Steve Edmunds and his wife.

"Nice one!" Sara grinned at the sight of his bare chest. She and Chris regularly hung out together. Their relationship was nothing too serious but in the confines of the small village they saw a lot of each other.

He returned the grin. "To what do I owe the honour of this visit?" He followed her back into the sale's area, still carrying his damp shirt in his hand.

Sara glanced around the shop at the stock of antiques but she had seen all of them before on her frequent visits. Her attention quickly returned to her friend. "Do I need a reason to come and visit you? Aren't you pleased to see me?"

"Of course, but I've already had the pleasure of the law calling on me so I was hoping this time it would be a paying punter. I suppose you'll have to do!"

"The law? What have you been up to?"

"Nothing really. I had a clock in the window, that appears to be a stolen one. The police took it away with them."

She raised her eyebrows. "Stolen goods?"

"So, it seems. But then in this business it's always a possibility. Anyway, I am busy and could do without all these interruptions. Especially as you don't want to buy anything."

She slapped him playfully across his bare arm then pulled him towards her for a hug. When they finally parted, Sara ran her fingers over a small tattoo, which she had noticed high on his right arm. "Is that from when you were in the Paras?" She scrutinised the regimental badge closely: the parachute depicted between two wings with a crown on the top. Below the badge were some initials. She read them out

33

aloud. "S.F.S.G. What does that stand for?"

Chris shrugged his shoulders. "Special Forces Support Group. When I was in Iraq we supported the American Marines."

Sara's eyes widened. "Special forces? Is that something like the SAS?"

He shrugged again; he was a little embarrassed. His army days were behind him, and best forgotten. He frowned at her question. "I suppose so. But that was in the past. I left the army a good ten years ago. It's not important now." He turned abruptly to go back to the workshop and the cabinet. It was paid for and the customer was waiting for it to be delivered. He'd already lost a day with his trip to help Steve Edmunds.

"Hang on a minute. I didn't mean to embarrass you. I only came to ask you to put this poster in your window for me." Sara unrolled the poster for him to see.

He took it from her and read it. "So. you've arranged another Folk Night at the pub, and I suppose you will be singing with your group..." He glanced at the line up for the folk night..." but who's this Derek Brown? I don't remember him from past concerts."

"You'll like him. He's a local young man from Brooke. He writes his own stuff and performs his songs to an acoustic guitar. He's been a big hit on You-tube. He's got thousands of followers online. I think he'll make it big one day soon."

Chris nodded non-committaly, his thoughts were already back with the Art Nouveau cabinet awaiting his attention in the workshop. He couldn't afford to waste such ideal weather for French-polishing.

"You will be coming, I hope? I do like your support on our Folk Nights." Sara pleaded.

He smiled at her and nodded. "Of course. Wouldn't miss it for the world." He took the poster and fixed it in the front window of the shop so anyone browsing the display would see it. "Now I must get on with some work. The cabinet I'm finishing is sold and the customer wants it delivered this week."

Sara said that she understood and went to the door. She turned and blew him a kiss before she let herself out into the bright sunlit street.

## Chapter Five

Early the next morning, Chris moved the lacquered clock, the small table and the writing slope into the workshop for restoration. He removed the movement from the clock and stored it safely until he could clean and check it over. The damaged lacquered clock case, he placed in the corner of the workshop awaiting his attention. He was pleased to find the tripod table just needed a clean and polish, which took him only a few minutes. When that was completed it was put straight into the front shop where it would be seen by the punters.

He checked the Art Nouveau cabinet he had completed restoring, and loaded it into his van intending to drive to Uppingham, to the home of the customer who had bought it. He was sure the woman would be pleased with the cabinet and the work he'd done on it. She liked the Art Nouveau period and her husband had asked him to keep an eye out for anything else in that style that she might fancy. Repeat customers like that were the backbone of a successful antique business.

When Chris arrived at the house in Uppingham he rang the front doorbell but couldn't make anyone hear. He cursed under his breath. He should have telephoned to check someone would be at home, but he'd failed to do that. He was about to get back in his van when he heard a voice calling from the back of the house. He opened the side gate and went towards the sound. In the secluded back garden he found the lady of the house stretched out on a sun lounger, completely naked! He retreated, apologising profusely as he turned away. "I'm sorry Mrs Gibbs. I didn't realise you were... sun bathing. I'll wait at the front while you dress."

"Hang on, don't run away." She removed her sunglasses and grinned at him. She made no attempt to cover herself. He couldn't help noticing that she was rather shapely. Although she was considerably older than him, she was still an attractive woman. The way she got up from her lounger left nothing to the imagination, but he was even more surprised when she came and grabbed his arm. "Don't be silly. I'm not embarrassed and I'm sure you've seen it all before. Do call me Veronica. Mrs Gibbs is so formal." She led him to the open patio doors and into the house.

"I'll get the cabinet for you. Where did you want it?" He tried to bring the conversation back to business.

She grinned again. "Where do I want what? That's the question." Her voice was quite deep and very suggestive.

He decided to ignore the hint. "The cabinet. You remember. I have an Art Nouveau cabinet in the van for you."

"Ah, my cabinet! I will want it putting in the hall."

He left her in the back room and went to the van. The cabinet was bulky but he always kept a sack barrow in his van for just such tasks. Chris wheeled the antique to the front door and pressed the doorbell.

"Come in." Veronica opened the door. She was standing out of sight behind it as she had still not bothered to get dressed.

He wheeled the cabinet into the hall and gently lowered it to the parquet floor. "Where exactly should I put it?"

Mrs Gibbs roared with laughter. He ample boobs giggled as she tried to control her mirth. "If you don't know where to put it by now, there's no hope for you at your age!"

The dealer felt his cheeks colour up. It was getting extremely embarrassing. She came over to him and put her arms around his neck. "I'm sorry Chris. I don't know what came over me. I will just pop upstairs and put on a dressing gown. Wait here...unless you'd like to come upstairs and help me?"

He shook his head. She was attractive enough but he knew her husband well. The man had bought a few things from him before, and mixing business with pleasure was not a good idea.

Veronica shook her head and frowned. "If I didn't know you better I would think you didn't like girls." With that loaded remark she made for the stairs.

He watched her walk seductively up the stairs, her bare bottom swaying at every step as she put on an exaggerated swagger. Five minutes later she was back downstairs dressed in a silk dressing gown.

"Now, where to place this Art Nouveau masterpiece?" She looked up and down the hall. "I think it will look best over there by the dining room doorway."

He lifted the cabinet and placed it where she had directed. He had to admit she was right. It did look very good there. They had a framed Mucha print hanging on the wall next to it. It looked as if that spot was made for it.

"Now, how much do we owe you?" Veronica looked as if butter wouldn't melt in her mouth; all thoughts of seduction seemed to have been forgotten.

He was relieved. He didn't fancy her, but he didn't want to upset a good customer. He'd tried to be tactful. Chris gave her the bill, which she glanced at, then placed on the cabinet top.

"It is a birthday present to me from my ever-loving husband." She explained. "Gerald will sort out the payment for you. Leave the account with me."

The dealer nodded. Mr Gibbs had intimated as much to him when he chose the cabinet and had specified a date for delivery before his wife's birthday. "You are a lucky lady, Mrs Gibbs. Your husband must love you a lot."

"Oh, he does, but I always think you can never have too much loving."

Back once more at his antique shop in Barrowick, Chris decided to tackle the Rosewood writing slope before he restored the lacquered clock case, as it needed the least work to get it into a saleable condition. He cleaned the old animal glue from the brass inlays, where they had sprung out of the box and was pleased to find he could re-use the original brass pieces once he had beaten them flat. He scored the underside

39

of the flatten&#2;d metal with coarse emery paper to give it a tooth, rubbed it over with a cut clove of garlic, a trick of the trade an old restorer had taught him, then glued it back into place. He placed the box under the workbench where it could rest undisturbed while the glue set.

Next, Chris turned his attention to the longcase clock. It was in a worse state than he had realised. It was obvious the whole of the case needed cleaning and restoring, and the lacquered panel on the base would have to be completely removed and rebuilt. He decided to go up to his flat, have a coffee and do some research in his illustrated clock books to find a suitable design. He needed to see an original clock of the same period to produce a convincing replacement panel. After some time searching his reference books he found just what he was looking for in a copy of English Domestic Clocks by Cescinsky and Webster. While he was searching through his collection of clock books, he checked in Baillie for any record of Jane Cooper: Baillie is the standard reference book of antique clock makers but even it can't possibly list every maker. As he had anticipated, Jane Cooper wasn't there. He knew it was a long shot, but he was intrigued by the name and just had to try to find her. He did find several male clock makers with the name of Cooper who were producing clocks in London at the correct period but he had no way of telling if one of them was Jane Cooper's husband.

The dealer knew that lacquer clocks of this period were invariably decorated with Chinese scenes. Some were very elaborate. Some dealers believed the blank wooden clock cases were sent by ship to China to be decorated with the lacquer work then returned by sea to England to be used in the clock

40

trade. This would have taken many months at sea. He was doubtful about this idea.

Finally, he found just what he was looking for. The design for the new panel used some of the motives he could see on the existing clock door, so the new design would match the case perfectly. He was just pinning a sheet of paper onto the drawing board to copy the design when the shop doorbell rang. He ran down the stairs and found one of his regular customers in the showroom. It was the Reverend John Smyth, the retired clergyman who took the occasional services at Barrowick church.

The village church overlooked Rutland Water and was built on a raised area of land reputed to be an ancient Barrow; that's how the village got its name. Wick was an old name for a farmstead and Barrow referred to the ancient burial mound. In the past the church would have been the centre of the village but now it was little used. Now there was just the occasional christening or wedding and a monthly Sunday service held by the Reverend Smyth and attended by a few local stalwarts like Sara Goodacre's mother. When John had business at the church, he often called at the antique shop, as he was an avid collector of antique oak pieces. He especially liked carved oak from old church pews and other fittings.

"Hello John. Nice to see you again." The dealer shook hands with the visitor. The vicar was a good customer and he was always welcome.

"Morning Chris. How are you? How's business?"

"Good. Thank goodness I keep finding items to restore and sell to keep the business ticking over."

"Ah! So what have you found recently?" The vicar

41

rubbed his hands together in anticipation.

"A longcase clock, but it's much too tall for your cottage." John Smyth lived near Oakham in an old cottage with low ceilings, which were only just over seven feet high. Chris knew of people who lived in such cottages and did have tall grandfather clocks but they were usually family pieces they did not wish to part with. Some clock owners even had a part of their house floor lowered to accommodate them, but John was definitely not a lacquer clock man, he was much more an old oak buyer.

"I saw a rather nice bracket clock in your window when I came over to take a christening service the other morning. I see it's gone already. Has it been sold?"

"Sorry, John. That one has gone already but I have some new items in the workshop. Apart from the longcase clock, I have a side table and I'm also restoring an inlaid Victorian writing slope. It's not the usual old oak that you collect, so I doubt you'd be interested."

"I don't know about that. I have always fancied a writing slope. What's the wood?"

"Nice rich Rosewood. It has brass inlays but they have sprung out so I'm gluing them back in."

Much to the dealer's surprise, John showed an interest in the item. "Can I see it? I have always fancied a nice antique writing slope."

"Of course. Come through into the workshop. I'm working on it at the moment." Chris took the box from under the bench and placed it on the top where the vicar could caste his knowledgeable eye over it.

"Nice one, Chris. I suppose the leather interior is in good

42

condition?"

"As far as I'm aware, John, but I haven't touched that yet. I wanted to get the exterior finished." He opened the box lid to show the interior.

"I like it. Give me first refusal when it's done." The vicar walked back into the showroom and glanced around. "Any bits of old oak?"

"No. You know I would have telephoned you if I had anything I thought you might like."

John smiled and slapped the dealer on the shoulder. "Good. It's nice having someone in the trade that I can trust to keep an eye out for me." He made for the door intending to walk over to the church. As he opened the door he turned and reminded the dealer. "Don't forget Christopher, I want first refusal on that writing slope." Then he was gone.

Chris returned to the workshop and took the clamps off the Rosewood box. With the brass inlays securely held in place, he needed to check for any other faults. Happily, the interior of the box was in excellent condition. The leather was pristine and well decorated with gold leaf motives; being protected from the daylight it had retained its original colour. He sprung the secret drawer that most writing slopes seem to have, but found nothing hidden inside it, then he checked the lid to see if it would need the French polish freshening. As he inspected the lid he particularly noticed the escutcheon in the centre of it. Someone had recently had two initials engraved on it. The letters R W were written in a fresh fancy script. As the engraved lettering was modern, he realised that it must stand for Richard Wilson, the late owner of the box. He ran his fingers over the brass shield and was surprised to feel it moved slightly under his touch.

"Damn! Another gluing job." He complained out loud. These small jobs all added up and the time spent sorting them out ate into his profit. He took a fine pointed tool and carefully prised the escutcheon from the box lid. To his surprise, it took very little persuading to come out.

Usually the lids of such boxes were made of a solid piece of wood, in this case Rosewood, but once he'd removed the brass plate he saw there was a hollow space inside the lid. The lid was constructed of two layers of wood with a space left between them. This was very unusual and intriguing. He tapped his knuckle on the wooden top and found it did indeed have a hollow ring to it. Careful inspection of the inner piece of wood revealed it was a recent addition. The craftsman who added it had stained it to match the old wood but to a trained yes there were tell-tale signs of the work. He tapped the lid again, intrigued by the hollow drum-like sound it emitted and realised the space would be an ideal place to hide a small document or something similar. It was the first time he had met a writing box with that particular hiding place built into it. Writing slopes regularly have secret drawers, hiding places under the pen slope or in the base of the box; some had several such secret places. He had checked for these already, but a hollow lid was new to him. He placed the box on the workbench and fetched a pen torch from the kitchen upstairs.

When Chris peered into the narrow hollow he was intrigued to see the end of a piece of white chord. Taking some tweezers, he pulled the chord out and was even more surprised to find a ribbon was attached to it. When he pulled

44

that out of its hiding place he saw it was not a smooth ribbon. It had a row of small raised bumps in it. He ran his fingers over the protrusions and held the ribbon up to the light to see if he could make out what was inside it. Unable to tell what the raised areas were from this perfunctory inspection, he took a scalpel and cut one of them out of its fabric covering.

The dealer was amazed at what he found. There on the palm of his hand he held what seemed to be a small piece of polished glass. He held it up between his fingers and took it to the light of the window. Once he had a better look at it, it dawned on him the transparent stone was faceted like a cut diamond! Must be glass, he thought, one of those cut-glass crystals they use in costume jewelry, but he had nagging doubts. Why would anyone take all that trouble to hide a worthless glass stone? He went back to the ribbon, ran his fingers over it and was surprised at what he could feel. There were a further nine small bumps remaining in the ribbon, making a possible ten stones in all, and some of the bumps felt larger than the one he had just removed from its hiding place. He rotated the single stone between his fingers, held it up to the window and viewed the daylight passing through it. There was no doubt the cut stone refracted the light much more intensely than he would expect from ordinary glass. He began to suspect he could have found a hoard of diamonds! If that was the case, it could be worth a small fortune! Carefully, he cut the remaining stones from their hiding place and took them up to his flat to inspect them. After some time examining his find and trying to understand just what he had stumbled upon, he placed them in an eggcup for safekeeping.

Chris made himself a coffee and sat in his favourite chair

by the French windows, looking out over Rutland Water and turning recent events over in his mind. This windfall took some understanding. He knew he would have to get an expert opinion on the stones. It was unbelievable that they would prove to be diamonds but why else would they be so well hidden? If they were gemstones, their value depended on all sorts of criteria used in the jewelry trade. He realised then why the two men might have been pushing Steve around outside his shop in Cley and asking after the antiques that had come from Richard Wilson's household. They must have known that Richard Wilson had these diamonds and they suspected he had hidden them somewhere in his antique furniture.

He wondered if the dead man's friends suspected he'd used the lid of the box to hide the diamonds. The two men hadn't asked specifically after the writing slope so maybe they weren't aware of the exact hiding place of the hoard, only that it could be in a piece of furniture. He guessed they had already searched Wilson's house and drawn a blank.

This recent find raised many more questions than answers. He put the eggcup with its contents into the kitchen cupboard while he considered what to do with them, then he went down to the workshop and turned his attention to the writing slope.

The slope's false lid had been specially made by fixing a new layer of wood inside it, leaving a space between it and the original top. He checked it carefully and discovered the new piece of wood was actually a layer of Rosewood veneered plywood. That kind of modern material had no place in an antique writing slope. This discovery went against his love of antiques and had to be rectified before he could bring himself to display and sell the box. It would never do to get a reputation for using plywood in his restoration work; serious antique collectors were fastidious about such things. He removed the layer of plywood and restored the box to its original construction. At the same time he replaced the brass escutcheon, which had been recently engraved with the owner's initials, substituting it with a plane piece of sheet brass. Any new owner could now have their initials engraved on the box, making it more personal. Small things like that made a difference to an item's saleability.

Later that day, having completed the restoration of the writing slope, he telephoned the Reverend Smyth to let him know it was ready for sale.

The vicar was very keen to see the finished job and called at the shop that same evening to inspect it. "Right, Christopher, let's see this writing slope."

The dealer brought the box through to the front shop and placed it on a table where John could open it and check it over.

"Nice slope. I do like the depth of colour and the rich grain in this Rosewood lid. I love the green tooled leather interior. I see the brass escutcheon is new. Was the original one missing?"

"The escutcheon was loose and it had been recently engraved, so I replaced it. I thought any purchaser might like to personalise the box with his own initials. I still have the old one and can fix it in the lid, if that's what you'd like."

"No. That's very sensible, Chris. I know most buyers would prefer what you've done. I certainly would." After a full inspection, the vicar closed the lid of the box and turned to the dealer. "Right, I'll take it. How much?"

Chris was pleased with this result. "I can do it for two hundred, as it's you. "

Without hesitation, John wrote out a cheque and carried the box out to his car.

Chris took the cheque upstairs to his flat and placed it in his wallet for safe keeping until he could get to the bank to deposit it. While he was up in the kitchen he couldn't resist another look at the stones he had found inside the box lid. He was still amazed at the unlikely circumstances that had led to the find. He'd bought the writing slope to help out an old friend. He'd noticed the escutcheon was loose and had removed it only to see the string underneath. That had led to removing the ribbon from the box and finding the diamonds, if indeed they did prove to be diamonds. It was an unlikely string of events, but it had happened!

He knew he would have to let an expert see the stones to be sure of their value so he decided to go and see Tania Wilkes at Uppingham the very next day Tania was a jewelry maker who sometimes worked with precious stones. Her studio was in an old farmhouse just outside Uppingham on the Stockerston Road. She was an old friend and he knew she could be trusted.

## Chapter Six

Next morning Chris called at the bank to pay in John Smyth's cheque then continued on to Uppingham to see Tania Wilkes. Tania and he had become acquainted through the antique business. He sometimes bid on her behalf at auctions if she fancied some antique jewelry she'd seen in the sale catalogue but didn't want to be bothered to attend the sale. The arrangement suited them both, as he would have attended the sales anyway to buy furniture and Tania preferred to be in her workshop crafting new pieces of jewelry or repairing old ones. She did regularly return the favour by buying pieces of jewelry from him that he had come by in his dealings. She was a firs- class jeweller, but he suspected she was too shy to bid at auction. At her Uppingham craft studio he found Tania at work melting silver in a small crucible and pouring it into a mould to make a brooch in a Celtic design.

"Hello Chris. What brings you out here?" Tania put down her crucible and removed her safety goggles.

"I need an expert opinion."

"Sounds intriguing. What have you brought? Some antique jewelry for me to see?"

He shook his head and took a small folded piece of paper from his wallet. Handing the paper carefully to Tania he said "I have come by two diamonds, or rather I think they are diamonds. They may just be cut glass but they look good to me. I wanted you to take a look at them for me and maybe value them."

Tania looked intrigued. "Diamonds! That's not your usual field."

"Exactly. That's why I brought them to you."

He had brought only two of the stones he had found in the writing slope, an example of the smallest and one of the largest of the hoard.

Tania put a loupe in her eye and took the largest stone to a strong desk-light she used for close work. She inspected the stone for some time then she took the smaller stone from the folded paper and inspected it. Finally, she folded the stones back into their paper cover and took the magnifying eyepiece off. Her smile told him the news was positive.

"Very nice stones, Chris. I don't know what you paid for them but they are diamonds and they are valuable".

He grinned. "Tell me about them."

"I'm not a diamond expert and can only draw on my limited experience of them, but for what it's worth, I'll give you my opinion."

"One thing's certain, Tania, you know a lot more about them than I do. I'm more a furniture and clock dealer. In fact, I've never had loose diamonds through my hands before these."

"I'll try and give you an idea of their worth. Diamond values depend on the four 'C's, that's clarity, cut, colour and carat weight."

He shrugged his shoulders because he was only vaguely following what she was explaining.

She continued. "Clarity is the absence of flaws in the stone. Most diamonds have inclusions in them but often they are so small you can only see them with a magnifying glass. Your two stones are completely clear, which is rare. Perfectly clear diamonds are the most valuable."

"Good."

"Ah! but that's not the end of it. The colour matters. These stones are absolutely colourless and bright. They have been cut recently, probably in Amsterdam by the beautiful workmanship. A Diamond Cutter shapes the facets of each stone to get the maximum amount of light refracted through it. That's what makes them glow. These are good."

"You think these stones have been well cut then?"

"Expertly cut. Now the final 'C', the carat weight, I estimate that the larger one is about two and a half carats and the smaller one only half a carat less. They are beautiful, top quality stones, Chris. I wish I'd bought them, but I couldn't afford them anyway."

"That's the million-dollar question, Tania. What do you think they are worth?"

"In today's market, where investors are buying gold and precious stones as a hedge against inflation, the price is at an all-time high. I would think..." She hesitated and went over to a pile of catalogues she had on top of her filing cabinet. She leafed through the pages of an auction catalogue from a recent sale held in the Birmingham jewelry quarter. "Let's say as a conservative estimate the larger stone is worth about £7,000 and the smaller one about £4,000. But you can't hold me to that valuation. You'll need to see an expert to be sure."

Chris whistled in surprise and sat down on the chair at Tania's desk.

She smiled at him. "From your reaction, I guess you didn't pay anything like that amount for them."

"I wasn't even sure they were diamonds." He shook his head in amazement.

Tania went over to her sink and filled the kettle. "Coffee?"

He just nodded, dumbstruck by her assessment of his find. With the other stones he had left in the eggcup in the kitchen cabinet, he guessed he had at least £50,000 to £60,000 worth of diamonds!

When he'd drunk the coffee and had time to digest the good news, he folded the diamonds carefully into the paper and replaced them in his wallet.

Tania was thrilled for him. "That will help pay the bills. Just think perhaps £11,000 in just two small pieces of compressed carbon. It's a strange world, isn't it? We shovel carbon on the fire as coal or coke but when it's been compressed in a volcano it's worth a fortune."

He was thrilled. £11,000 sounded good but the total value was amazing. He thought about the circumstances of his windfall. Having that amount of loose stones was ridiculous unless you were in the wholesale diamond business. As far as he was aware, the late Mr Richard Wilson wasn't known as a jewelry dealer so why had he hidden such a valuable cache in the lid of the writing slope? Ten to one it was a scam of some sort, of that he was certain. He began to feel uneasy about keeping such valuable things in the kitchen cupboard and decided he would put them in a bank safe deposit box at the first opportunity. He also decided he would share this windfall with Steve Edmunds as Steve needed some financial help and he had been the unwitting purchaser of that very valuable writing slope in the first place.

All the way back to Barrowick, Chris kept thinking about his good fortune. It was such a long shot. If Steve hadn't bought the box; if he hadn't bought it to help Steve out; if he hadn't noticed the loose escutcheon and remove it, by now the diamonds would be in the vicar's writing slope and John Smyth wouldn't have a clue they were there! Sometimes fate seemed to play a blinder of a hand! That find certainly made up for the time spent and the work on the lacquered clock.

Back at his flat, he wrapped eight of the diamonds in tissue paper and put them into a silver card case he had in stock. The two stones that Tania had valued he intended taking to the post office to send to Steve. He wrote a quick note to Steve to be included with the consignment and placed it in an envelope with the diamonds, then he went to the bank in Oakham and had the silver card case containing his diamonds, put into a strong box. Later, at the post office on Oakham High Street, he sent the diamonds by secure post to Steve at Cley.

When he arrived home, he telephoned Steve to explain to him what was happening. "Steve? It's Chris. You OK are you? No more unwanted visitors?"

"No. I think you frightened them off."

53

"Good, I have some good news for you. I have just posted a valuable parcel to you. You should get it tomorrow. You'll have to sign for it so make sure you're at home."

Steve fell silent taking his time digesting this information.

Finally, Chris asked. "You still their mate? "

"Yes, sorry. I thought you said something about a valuable parcel. What have you done now?"

"Don't sound so shocked. I'll explain. You remember that writing slope I bought from you."

"Yes, of course. You haven't sold it for a fortune, have you?"

"No, not exactly. When I came to restore it, I found a hidden chamber in the lid. It contained some diamonds. "

"Diamonds! Bloody hell!"

"I have just posted two of those stones to you by secure mail. They are estimated to be worth about £11,000."

The phone line went silent again.

"You still there, Steve? Not fainted, have you?"

"No. No. I'm just lost for words. I'm speechless!"

Chris went on to explain how he'd found the diamonds hidden in the writing slope by accident. He didn't tell Steve how many he'd found but he did explain that the two stones posted to him were worth at least £11,000 on the wholesale market.

Steve was amazed and dumbstruck. The telephone line fell silent again.

"You still there?"

"Yes. How come you found diamonds in that writing slope. I checked the secret drawers myself and I'll swear they were empty. Where were they?"

"They were concealed in the lid, which was hollow. I have had them valued by a friend in the jewelry trade so I'm fairly confident of my facts. Tell me, did you know Richard Wilson dealt in precious stones?"

"No, not him! He was known locally as a bit of a wide boy but no one knew for sure how he got his money. If he had diamonds stashed away you can bet it was certainly not legit."

"That's what I thought. I think we had better keep stum about where the diamonds were found. If Wilson was up to something shady, the diamonds won't be missed and we can cash them in."

Steve thanked his friend profusely for cutting him in on the deal. That windfall would help him over a rough period in his business. "You really are a mate, Chris. I don't know how we can ever thank you enough."

"That's what mates are for." Chris put down the telephone, pleased with his good deed.

Later that evening he returned his attention to the design for the lacquered clock base. He copied the outline of a Chinese scene he'd found in his clock book, adding a few of the elements pictured on the Jane Cooper clock door. He added a bridge, two blossom trees and a robed figure to the picture as these repeated elements would tie the trunk door and the new base design together, giving them more authenticity.

The dealer enjoyed working on the new design. He had worked on replacement lacquer work before when he'd restored an eighteenth century Tavern Clock. At that period Lacquered clocks and furniture had been very popular. There was a fashion for such elaborate Chinoiserie furniture in the mid 1700's when the Jane Cooper clock was made. Satisfied with his new design, he took it down to his workshop to check it fitted the base correctly. When he had time, he would remove the damaged lacquer from the base and transfer his design onto it. If he could restore the clock and match the original lacquered finish on the door, so that it was impossible to distinguish the new part from the old, he knew he could ask over £1500 for the clock. That way he would get his money back, but that small profit paled into insignificance when he considered the value of the diamonds sitting in the bank strong room.

## Chapter Seven

Sara Goodacre and Chris were both very busy the rest of that week. Apart from seeing her when he went to the pub for his mid-day meal, they saw nothing of each other socially. He was busy restoring the lacquered clock and Sara was engrossed in planning one of her regular folk nights that she organised for the Barrowick Arms.

On Wednesday, the day Sara was holding her folk night, Chris spent the day working in the back shop. That morning Gerald Gibbs called to pay for the Art Nouveau cabinet that had been delivered to his wife in Uppingham.

"Lovely piece of work, Chris. Very well preserved for its age."

The dealer couldn't help thinking Gerald might just be referring to his wife!

"Veronica was thrilled with the delivery. She told me you caught her sunbathing and were a bit embarrassed. You needn't be. We are both very broad minded."

57

Chris wasn't sure where this conversation was leading. He didn't reply.

Gerald continued in a conspiratorial voice. "You shouldn't be embarrassed by Veronica. She and I lead separate lives as far as sex is concerned. In fact, she's a bit of a nympho since she passed the menopause, and I can't keep up with her. A young chap like you might be doing me a favour." He winked wickedly and nudged the dealer's arm.

Chris wasn't sure what to say. He didn't want to offend Gerald as he was a good customer and he hadn't yet paid for the cabinet, but he knew playing with Veronica would be playing with fire. He grinned sheepishly.

"Anyway lad, here's the cheque for the cabinet. Veronica says she will call here in the near future to see what else you can do for her."

That promise of more trouble with Gerald's wife was not lost on the dealer. "I'll have to see what her tastes are...in antiques of course. Then I can look out for pieces she might like."

Gerald nodded enthusiastically. "Good lad. I'll tell her she's welcome any time."

The dealer watched the man leave the shop and get into his Jaguar car. The Gibbs were trouble, but business was business. He couldn't afford to turn away such good payers. Maybe he could tell Sara what was happening and get her to drop everything and come to his rescue if he called her. Then again, maybe Sara wouldn't want to know he'd been alone with Veronica Gibb when she was naked. She certainly hadn't liked it when Vickie, his ex-wife had turned up at his shop and stripped off to persuade him to take up with her again.

58

Sometimes a bloke didn't know what to do for the best!

When time for the evening folk event arrived, Chris showered and changed from his grimy work clothes and went along to the pub to support Sara, as he had promised. There was already a good crowd there when he arrived. He found a place near the bar at the back of the room and sat on a high stool so he had a good view over the heads of the other customers. He made sure he could see all of the small stage.

Derek Brown, the young man that Sara had mentioned was a hit on YouTube, was performing on stage when he arrived at the gig. He was good. He accompanied himself on acoustic guitar and sang some of his own compositions. The audience clapped loudly, some even voiced their appreciation when he finished his act.

As Sara was nowhere to be seen, Chris assumed she was getting ready for her own turn on stage. Meanwhile, the bar was run by Sara's mother, with help from a young man that he recognised as Sara's cousin. After a few minutes the lad came to serve him.

"Yes Sir?"

"A pint of bitter, and I'll have a packet of crisps as I'm feeling a bit peckish."

The barman served him then carried on serving the other customers. Sara's mother came over to him and passed the time of day with him. She had been dead set against his relationship with her daughter as Chris was a divorced man and Mrs Goodacre was rather religious, but time and circumstances had mellowed the woman's attitude and Sara had shown no signs of heeding her mother's warnings anyway.

"Where's Sara?" Chris asked.

"She'll be on in a minute. I think there is one member of the band missing. John, the guitarist, hasn't turned up yet."

"Oh dear!" He could well imagine the panic going on backstage. John was an important part of the small band, he was the lead guitarist.

Finally, Sara came on stage, took the microphone and apologised to the audience. "I'm afraid John, our lead guitarist, can't make it this evening, but Derek Brown has volunteered to step in as his las- minute replacement." She turned to welcome the band onto the stage and led the clapping for the young man who was set to save the evening.

Chris sat back and enjoyed the show. Sara was in good voice as usual and the replacement guitarist managed to play his was through most of the unfamiliar numbers without too much difficulty. After five numbers the band took a break. That was the signal for the audience to rush to the bar with their orders. The dealer sat back and watched them queuing three deep to get served.

After a few minutes Sara appeared behind the bar to help out. With her help, the crowd was soon served and dispersed to their seats. She eventually came to Chris and enquired if he wanted another beer.

"Yes please. You do seem to have another successful folk night on your hands. Mind you, you deserve it. The word has obviously got around the area what a fun night it can be here."

Sara grinned at this praise. She leaned over and thanked him for supporting her.

He asked her "What's happened to John? Any idea why he hasn't turned up?"

"I've just phone his home and a neighbour answered. It seems his wife has just been admitted to hospital as an emergency. Their second child is coming a bit early. That's much more important than our folk night."

"Best excuse yet!"

After the band finished playing for the night, the customers melted away and Mrs Goodacre called time on the late drinkers. Chris kissed Sara goodnight and left the pub where the band was having a celebratory drink after their successful night's work. Sara seemed very attentive to the young guitarist. She was thrilled he had helped make the evening a success and had turned a disaster into a triumph. She was talking animatedly to him and didn't notice Chris was departing for home.

The dealer set out to walk to his shop at the top of Main Street. By that time, it was dark and most of the cars had left the village but as he neared his home he noticed a solitary car parked outside his premises. As the street had been so busy earlier in the evening he thought nothing of this lone vehicle until it flashed its lights and sounded its horn very loudly. Suddenly, there was the sound of car doors slamming and the car engine revved loudly as it sped away towards the main road. It passed him doing at least fifty miles per hour down the narrow village street!

He quickened his pace; that action was very suspicious. As soon as he unlocked the front door of the shop and went inside, he felt an unfamiliar draft. From that unexpected movement of cooler air, he realised a window or door must be open somewhere on the premises, but he knew he'd locked and secured everywhere before he went to the folk night!

He switched on the lights and rushed through to the workshop. He was shocked to find the back door swinging on its hinges. It was badly damaged and wide open!

"Damn. A break in!" He cursed aloud as he ran to the back door and out into the darkened yard. No one was in sight, nothing moved apart from a neighbour's cat, scurrying away from him. There was no sign of life to be seen or heard in the area.

Chris went back into the shop and inspected the back door. It could be that someone had forced it open. They must have used a crowbar because the door was splintered and the lock was hanging off. It had been securely locked and bolted from the inside when the dealer left the premises. Chris shook my head in dismay. That mess would take some sorting out. He turned his attention to the workshop and the sales area to see what had been stolen.

A few things had been disturbed as the thief had obviously been in a hurry. The tripod table he had bought from Steve, was overturned in the front shop and the lacquered clock case was lying on the floor and no longer on the workbench where he had left it, otherwise the stock seemed to be undisturbed. His desk, in the corner of the workshop, had been ransacked, there were invoices and paperwork strewn all over the floor. That was a problem he didn't relish sorting. Filing all the invoices and paperwork would take ages, but he knew the intruders would have found nothing of value in the desk as he kept no money or valuables in there. He went up to his flat and was relieved to find no signs of disturbance there. He felt he had arrived just in time to prevent much more damage.

The dealer telephoned the police to report the burglary. The officer who took the call, checked with him if anything had been taken then gave him an incident number, otherwise he seemed uninterested in the problem. It seemed to be all in a night's work for him.

"We have a car in your area, Sir. They are attending an incident on the A1 at present. An officer will be with you soon. Leave everything as you found it, in case there are any clues to who broke into your premises."

With that promise the officer rang off and he was left to wait for the arrival of the duty policeman. He made a coffee and checked the shop stock again while he waited for the police to arrive. It was well after midnight by the time the squad car drew up outside the antique shop. Two police officers came in. One of them he recognised as the man who had removed the stolen bracket clock from his front window display.

"I thought Barrowick was a quiet backwater but it seems your business is prone to problems." The officer observed.

"It's not usually like this. This is my second bit of bad luck. I only hope my problems don't come in threes!"

After a brief look around and an assurance from Chris that nothing seemed to be missing, the officers took a statement and left him to clear up the mess. He decided to temporarily fix the back door by screwing it shut and nailing batons across it as it was getting very late by then. That quick job would have to do until the morning when he would make time to do a proper repair on it.

After he'd made the workshop secure, he went up to his flat and made himself a night drink. He sat in his favourite

63

chair near the French windows, considering the break in. From the items the burglars had handled it seemed they were only interested in the antiques Steve had sold him. Putting two and two together didn't take much effort. Whoever broke into the shop that night must have watched him leave for the folk night then forced the back door. That would have taken the burglars some time as it was a stout wooden door and they would have tried to work quietly. A lookout sat in the car parked outside and sounded the alarm when they spotted him leaving the pub and coming up Main Street. Further consideration convinced him the break in was no coincidence. It was obvious someone knew about the diamonds and was looking for their hiding place. They must have been familiar with Richard Wilson's furniture but didn't know which piece the man had used to hide the hoard. If they had known they would have just looked for the writing slope, which happily wasn't at the shop anymore.

Chris realised someone had found out he'd bought the items from Steve that he had purchased from Mrs Wilson. But how had they fingered him? He would have to contact Steve to see if someone had been indiscrete about the diamonds that he had posted to him. With all those thoughts churning around in his mind, he went to bed, but sleep eluded him.

In the small hours of the morning he got up and made himself another hot drink and stood at the French windows watching the full moon reflected on the still waters of the reservoir. Even when he eventually returned to his bed and had managed to nod off to sleep, his night was disturbed by vivid nightmares.

64

## Chapter Eight

First thing Thursday morning Chris had a telephone call from Steve.

"Dawn was thrilled with your gift, Chris. It will see us out of the financial fix we're in. Thanks again. By the way, the other antiques from Richard Wilson's house will come up for auction in the next few weeks. Our local antique sales are always held on a Wednesday. If you are interested in attending the sale I will let you know when, and I'll see you there."

Chris thanked his friend for the information then took a deep breath and broached the bad news. "Someone broke into my premises last night while I was at a folk evening at my local. They searched the workshop and shop looking for something. They didn't take anything but they did make a mess."

"Oh! Any idea who it was?"

"As a matter of fact, yes. It must have been someone like the two blokes who attacked you. Whoever broke into my shop checked only those items I bought from you. I think they were looking for the diamonds. I wonder if you or maybe Dawn has mentioned your windfall to anybody?"

Steve went very quiet.

Chris waited several seconds then asked, "Steve. You still there?"

"Yes. I certainly haven't said anything to anybody, but Dawn was at her WI meeting yesterday morning and she was terribly excited about your gift. Maybe she just let it slip."

Chris considered this possibility. "Well, the damage is done now, if she did blab to her friends it's too late to stop her. The cat is well and truly out of the bag."

"I'm so sorry, Chris." Steve sounded choked. "I'll have a word with her, but as you say, it's too late now to put the genie back into the bottle."

"While you are on the phone, Steve, let me give some advice. Get those diamonds stored somewhere safe. Put them somewhere secure like a bank vault. Luckily, I had already put mine in my bank so they wouldn't have found anything if they had turned the place completely upside down."

Steve readily agreed.

Chris signed off with a warning. "Do watch your back. If they will come all this way on the off chance and break into my shop, they may well soon be visiting you." He put the phone down and cursed myself for bringing Steve into the situation. Sometimes things he did for the best possible reasons turned sour on him.

To take his mind off the events of the previous night, he

set about the restoration of the lacquered clock case. He scraped the old lacquer from the base of the clock and sanded the Oak board to a smooth finish. Satisfied with that process, he sealed the bare wood with a layer of quick drying varnish. Once that was dry, he copied his drawing onto the base using Tracedown to provide a guide for the design then he built up the raised parts of the design with a mixture of fine chalk and the best animal glue. He copied the methods used by the old craftsmen and use well sieved chalk powder mixed with Rabbit skin glue, the finest grade available. Places like the heads of the figures and some of the larger tree trunks were coated with this mixture and made to stand out to give the design a three-dimensional effect. Once this layer of gesso was dry and sanded to shape, he painted it with grey undercoat then mixed gloss paints to try to match the finish of rest of the case. It was a difficult task but after several trial mixtures he was satisfied with his results.

The original clock case had been green lacquer but centuries of exposure to the detrimental effects of sunlight, open fires and dust had reduced the colour to a dull grey with only the faintest traces of the original green ground showing. By carefully mixing tube oil colour into grey gloss paint, he managed to reproduce the colour perfectly. Once the gloss layer was applied, he left the clock case to dry in the workshop. Later, when the gloss layer was perfectly dry, he would heighten parts of the design with gold leaf paint and then coat it with a matt varnish. This was a system he had devised and used to good effect many times before on antique lacquered items such as Tavern clocks, Chinese Screens or Chinoiserie corner cabinets. In the past he had put many of his restored lacquered pieces into antique auctions and they had sold well.

A few days previously, Chris had left some bids at an auction in the local saleroom in Stamford. As he needed to leave the clock case to dry undisturbed, it seemed a good opportunity to contact them to check if he had had any luck. There had been some wall clocks in the catalogue that interested him. When he telephoned the sale room he was pleased to hear he'd managed to get two of the clocks at a good price. With time on his hands, he decided it was an ideal opportunity to go to Stamford to pay for his purchases and pick them up.

The Stamford saleroom is very close to a retail park with several of the larger shops and with free parking. After he'd paid for his purchases and loaded them into his van, he parked in the nearby carpark and did a bit of shopping. He was just leaving Sainsburys with milk, some bread and other essentials when he came face to face with a familiar figure from his past.

"Vickie! What are you doing back in Stamford?" It was his ex-wife. They had parted on bad terms and he believed she had left the area. He was not pleased to bump into her and see she was back in the town.

Vickie must have seen the look of surprise and consternation on his face. She grinned at his unease. "Don't get upset, Chris, I am only visiting. I've come over for Tina's wedding."

Tina was an old friend of his ex's. They used to knock around together when Vickie was married to Chris and they lived in Stamford.

He recovered his composure. "Tina getting married? Good. And are you managing OK?"

"I'm fine. I've gone into partnership with a young chap in an antique business in Norwich."

"Good. I'm glad you've fallen on your feet." He actually wasn't really concerned about Vickie. She was the sort of girl who would survive anyway, even if she had to play dirty, as she had with him when they were married. He turned to go to his van. "Look after yourself." He called over his shoulder.

Meeting Vickie in Stamford brought back a few bad memories and some deep concerns. Chris was only too pleased to hear she was not returning to the area and he really was rid of her.

Back at the Barrowick shop, he checked the lacquered clock case and was pleased to find the gloss paint had dried sufficiently to carry on with the restoration. He fetched the clock book down from his flat and use it to fill in the details with gold leaf paint. As he worked, the Chinese scene grew in greater detail.

He kept referring to the door of the clock, which was highly decorated in the Chinoiseries manner of the mid 1700's, and tried to keep the new work true to the original. There were no customers to disturb him and the work went well. He was just cleaning his paint brushes and admiring the new base when the shop bell rang, announcing another punter.

When he went into the sales area he found a tall, well-dressed, man looking around the showroom. The customer had the air of a country squire about him; tweed jacket, plus fours and a tweed cap. The dealer asked if he could help.

The man knew exactly what he was looking for. "I want to buy an antique writing slope for my father. It's his 70th birthday next week and he's always wanted one."

Chris shook his head. "Sorry. I don't have one in stock. I do tend to concentrate on older antiques and not the Victorian period."

The man seemed surprised. "Oh! I was talking to a dealer in Cley only yesterday afternoon and he told me I had just missed a beautiful example. I understood he said he had sold it to you."

The dealer eyed the man thoughtfully. This was too much of a coincidence. He decided to play along with him. "Cley? Where's Cley? It's not a place I go buying antiques. It can't be round here or I would know it." He smiled and spread his hands in a gesture of regret that he couldn't help.

The customer seemed unhappy at this denial. He frowned and stroked his chin, which drew attention to a small white scar he had there. "I must have been mistaken then. Sorry to have troubled you." He made to go to the door then turned back and said. "If you do come by an inlaid Rosewood writing slope please keep it for me."

Chris was about to ask for his phone number or his address when the man jumped in his car and sped off leaving the dealer standing in the shop doorway staring down Main Street. He went back into the shop and sat down on a carver chair in the showroom. This was too much of a coincidence to be unconnected with the box he had bought from Steve and the recent burglary. He decided to telephone Steve again.

70

"Steve? It's Chris. Have you got a minute?"

Steve seemed pleased to speak to him. "I had a word with Dawn. I'm sure she told her friends at the WI that we had been given some valuable diamonds by you. She didn't exactly admit it, but she didn't deny it either. She went very quiet when I tackled her about it."

"I expected as much, Steve, but that's not why I rang you. There's been another development this afternoon."

"Oh!" Steve waited for the explanation.

"I've just had a chap in my shop asking me if I had a Rosewood writing slope in stock. He told me you said you had recently sold me one."

Steve spluttered down the phone. "Me! No way!"

"That's what I suspected. He was a country gent type of bloke. Wore plus fours and a tweed jacket. He spoke with a broad Norfolk accent..." He got no further before Steve interrupted him.

"Had he got a small scar on the left side of his chin?"

"Yes."

"That's an ex copper by the name of Barry Montgomery. He got that scar years ago trying to arrest a drunk who hit him with a bottle. Barry was one of Richard Wilson's closest cronies. I don't know what business they had in common but they were often seen together drinking in Holt. He's only a retired country copper. He never even made sergeant but he does like to play at being the country gent. "

"Thanks Steve. So, he's a friend of the Wilsons. That ties in with what I was thinking. Whoever is looking for those diamonds appears to suspect where they were hidden. With so much money at stake they will not give up easily. I hope

71

you've found a safe place t ) keep yours."

"I took them to m', bank this morning, just as you advised. I really could do with the money but I suppose I'd better lay low with them and not cash them in for the present. Maybe when you decide to sell your stones you could sell mine for me as well. I only hope that will not be too long because I could do with the cash right now."

"Oh dear! I'm sorry Steve, but you do see the sense in waiting? I was thinking we should let time pass and the search die down then I'll contact someone in the trade in Birmingham and get them sold in a precious stone auction where they'll be one lot among many and they won't arouse any undue interest."

When Chris came off the phone, he couldn't get the afternoon's events out of his mind. Whoever wanted the diamonds was not giving up easily. He would have to be very careful how he went about selling them when it eventually came to it. He was also concerned about the Reverend Smyth, who had bought the writing slope from him. If someone suspected the vicar had the item they may try to break in to his home. It was very unlikely the gang would find out that John had the slope but then he suddenly realised there was a record of that sale in his paperwork, and that had been disturbed during the break in. He immediately went into the workshop and searched through his sales invoices but he couldn't find the relevant paperwork anywhere. After a thorough search he realised that was the only invoice missing and it must have been taken. That paperwork would tell the thief who had purchased the writing slope as John Smyth's address would be on the invoice.

Chris was concerned at this unwelcome discovery and felt he owed it to the vicar to warn him. He telephoned John at home and was lucky enough to find him in.

"John? It's Chris Doughty at Barrowick Antiques."

"Hello Chris. What can I do for you?"

"I have had a problem or two since I bought that writing slope and one or two other antiques in Norfolk."

"Problems? What sort of problems?"

"There seems to be a lot of interest in that box."

"So? How does that affect me?"

The dealer could tell from John's tone of voice he was intrigued, and he knew the vicar was not easily fooled as he was used to dealing with people in his ministry. He chose his words carefully. "Your writing slope had a hollow lid. It was a secret hiding place for valuables, which was accessed via the escutcheon. Writing slopes usually have one or two secret drawers but this one was the first I've seen with a secret compartment in the lid. I did remove the second layer of wood when I restored the box, as the restoration wasn't correct for the period or up to my standard. They'd used plywood for the job."

"Interesting, but I suspect you are leading up to something else."

"I have had a break in at the shop and the burglars were only interested in some antiques I bought along with that box. The only items disturbed were a longcase clock and a table. Both came from the same source as the writing slope."

"I see."

"This morning I had a chap with a broad Norfolk accent asking if I had any writing slopes.   It seems he contacted the

73

dealer in Cley that sold the writing slope to me."

"Even more interesting. Tell me, when you found the hollow in the lid did you find anything of value in it? Maybe a document or deed? It does seem someone has an unusual interest in that item."

Chris hesitated, not wishing to share with anyone else the details of the diamonds. "No John. Whatever was there must have been removed before I bought the box. As you say, it was a narrow space and probably housed some document or other." There was a few seconds silence before John Smyth spoke again and the dealer felt the vicar was suspicious of his answer, but it could just have been his guilty conscience.

"Well thanks for telling me, Chris. I will not be showing the slope to all and sundry so there's only you and I know I bought it from you. "

"That's good. But the thief took some of my invoices and yours was among them. I felt you should be aware of the interest in the writing slope. I wouldn't want you getting burgled because of it." The dealer rang off and considered his position. John Smyth was a good customer and a good friend. He just had to warn him about the burglary, but he deliberately hadn't mentioned the diamonds, the real reason for the interest in the Rosewood box. Unfortunately, the dealer's concern for the vicar proved correct.

## Chapter Nine

Three days after the break-in at the antique shop Chris was working on a wall clock in his back shop. It was a three weight Vienna Regulator he had bought from a runner who called on him on the off chance he might do some business.

Chris didn't bother with the run of the mill regulators, the ones that were spring driven and frequently came up for sale. They were poor time-keepers, made cheaply to provide the Victorian working masses with a means of getting to work on time. The clock he purchased, was weight driven and would keep accurate time once it was fully restored. The three weights, which hung on gut chords in the case, provided power for the time, for striking the hours and playing a musical strain on the quarters and the hour.

When he stripped the movement to clean and restore it, he was thrilled to find the clock was manufactured by the Lenzkirch company. It bore the Austrian firm's name and their Laurel leaf logo on its back plate. This was a welcome find. Lenzkirch clocks were manufactured at Baden near the Swiss border and were considered among the best of their kind. They were so highly regarded there was a gallery dedicated to them in the Austrian Museum of Decorative Arts in Vienna.

The Lenzkirch factory started working in 1860 and closed in 1932. Clock collectors value the fine movements and cases and are willing to pay a premium to possess one of those clocks. When he bought the clock from the runner, Chris had recognised it as a good example of a wall clock from the quality of wooden case. To find it was a Lenzkirch was an added bonus.

He took the movement apart and immersed the parts in horological cleaning solution while he inspected the case. The wood used to make the case was a nicely grained Walnut. It was a good coloured, decorative example, of that hardwood. Walnut is prone to woodworm infestation but thankfully there was no sign of woodworm damage, however, some of the old French-polish needed removing and renewing as the daylight had faded it and made it cloudy. He stripped the old finish with fine wire-wool and methylated spirit before he renewed the layer of polish.

The clock movement was reassembled. It had just needed cleaning and oiling; there were no worn bushes to replace in the plates and no worn or broken teeth or pinions on the wheels. He was thrilled with it and knew it would sell for a good profit. He had just placed it on his workshop wall to regulate it when he had an unexpected visitor. The Reverend John Smyth called at the shop.

When the doorbell sounded Chris washed his hands and went into the display area at the front of the building. "John, nice to see you again. What can I do for you?"

The vicar came right to the point of his visit. "It's about that writing slope I bought from you."

"Problems? I'll gladly fix it if I can."

"I'm afraid it's more serious, Christopher, it was stolen, just as you warned me it may be."

Chris was completely taken aback at this disclosure. "From your house? Have you had a burglary? "

"Yes. Two nights ago, when we were out at a dinner, someone broke into the back of the house by forcing the lock on the French windows, which overlook the back garden."

"Did you lose much?"

"No, thank goodness. Whoever broke in didn't realise the value of my antique Oak collection. All they took was the writing slope. Luckily, I'd left it in full view on a table near the window."

The dealer swore silently, under his breath. The last thing he wanted was to involve his customers in his problems. "I am sorry. What a nuisance."

The vicar could see his friend's concern. "Don't blame yourself Chris. Don't take it to heart. I am well insured and you did warn me there might be some unexpected interest in that box."

"Yes, but it's not fair on you to bring that kind of problem to your door. I can't apologise enough. You must be devastated at being burgled."

John smiled. "I was a curate in one of the roughest areas of East London when I first became a priest. We were broken into regularly in those days; in fact we became suspicious when it stopped for a month or so. That's why I have always been well insured. Anyway, after my conversation with you, I decided to leave the box ih full view of the door, where it could be seen. I thought anyone looking for it would find it easily then leave everything else alone. It seems it was the right strategy. I was proved right."

"You certainly understand people, John. That's not something I would have thought about."

The dealer was relieved at the vicar's positive attitude but he still felt guilty at the way he had involved him. "I'd better look out for a replacement writing slope for you. That's the least I can do. I'm sure I can find you a similar one. They do come up at auction fairly frequently."

"No need. The thief took my box, removed the brass escutcheon from the lid then threw it into the hedge at the bottom of my garden. I have it in the car. I came over to ask you to repair it for me."

"Well, it's obvious they were looking for something that they thought was hidden in that lid and they wouldn't have found it. I told you the top was originally hollow but there was nothing hidden in it. I removed the plywood liner and restored the box to its original state, so they wouldn't even have found a hollow in the lid."

"Yes, you did explain that to me. Whatever had been hidden in that lid must be very valuable for us both to be burgled because of it."

Chris frown and made no further comment.

John looked at this friend, holding his gaze just a little too long for the dealer's comfort, making him feel guilty and under suspicion. Chris looked down at his feet and coloured up.

The vicar turned to leave the shop. "I have the box in the

car. I will bring it in for you to repair it for me."

The dealer took a deep breath and composed himself. The vicar was no fool and was used to reading people. He felt very exposed but he tried not to show it. When John brought the box into the shop he could see the damage that had been done. Someone had used a knife or something similar to force the brass plate from the lid. Luckily the damage was not extensive and the lid was easily restorable. "I'll do it free of charge for you, John. I feel guilty you were ever involved in this business."

"No need for that, Christopher. The insurance will pay for it as well as the repairs to my French Windows. It's about time I had a return on my annual outlay to them. This is the first claim I've made in years. Give me a ring when the job's done and let me have an invoice to claim the money back."

"That's very fair of you. Thanks. While I have the box and as I'm going to fit a new escutcheon to it, would you like me to get your initials or name engraved on it? That will make it more personal."

"That's a nice idea. Just get the initials J.S. put on it. That will be enough for me. Now I must get across to the church. I have a christening later today and the font needs to be filled."

Chris escorted the vicar to the door. "Are you sure there's nothing else I can do for you?" He asked

John hesitated in the doorway. "Yesterday I saw an antique Oak carving of the Green Man. Unfortunately, it wasn't for sale otherwise I would have had it"

"Was that local?"

"No. It was on a misericord in a church in Ludlow. It was a Beautiful example of oak carving from the mid 1400's. "

"Well I've never seen one in the antique trade, so your best bet is to carry a saw with you when you visit those churches." Chris joked.

"Even I wouldn't remove a piece from a church pew; especially from there. The incumbent was once a curate of mine and is an old friend." He smiled at the thought of the situation. "I have several carved pieces from medieval churches but I've never managed to find one of the Green Man. Keep an eye out for me, please."

"I will, but I've never come across one before."

John made for the door. "I must go now. Let me know when I can pick up my writing slope."

The dealer watched the vicar cross the road to his church. It struck him as curious that a devout Christian would be looking for a pagan carving like the Green Man. That figure was occasionally found in Christian churches but was from a much older religious belief, when ancient men worshipped deities closer to nature and the seasons were thought to be under the rule of their Gods. The Arthurian legends mention the Green Knight and his ability to regenerate each spring as nature itself did. That was just another example of the ancient Green Man myth.

Once John Smyth was out of sight, Chris returned to business. He took the Lenzkirch clock from his workshop and placed it on the wall in his display window. It replaced the Edwardian bracket clock taken by the police. He did like to remind the punters he dealt in antique clocks, as he so loved restoring them. Back in the workshop he removed the lid from the Rosewood writing slope and assessed the damage. Luckily the brass escutcheon had come out clean with minimal damage to the surrounding wood. He decided to fit a slightly larger brass plate as a replacement so he could remove the slight damage to the Rosewood, which had surrounded it. He carefully enlarged the area where the plaque would fit then took a rubbing of it to act as a template for the new piece of brass.

In the oddments drawer in his workshop there were several small pieces of engraving brass, a metal rich in Lead, which made it ideal for engraving sharp line. A search among these pieces soon found him one that could be cut to size. With the template transferred to the brass sheet, he cut the shape using a piercing saw then cleaned the edges with a fine file. As the vicar wanted his initials engraved on the new escutcheon, he went online and printed a decorative J and S in the correct size font. Those initials were transferred onto the plaque using tracedown paper.

The dealer had perfected his engraving skills when he repaired some clock works and was quite capable of successfully engraving two capital letters onto the brass sheet. Doing it himself with a gravure saved him time and expense and got the box restored and back to the vicar as quickly as possible.

He placed the escutcheon blank on a leather pouch filled with fine sand, and engraved the vicar's initials. Half an hour later he had polished the brass plaque and it was ready to be glued back into the lid. He held the plaque up to the light and was pleased with his work. It was useful having so many skills; it meant he could save time and money by not putting such jobs out to other craftsmen. He glued the new brass escutcheon into the Rosewood lid and replaced the lid onto the box. All he needed to do to complete the job was touch up the French polish around the new brass plate. Next day he would ring John Smyth and tell him his writing slope was repaired and awaiting collection.

## Chapter Ten.

A few weeks after the burglaries at the Barrowick antique shop and the vicar's home, when things seemed to have quietened down, Chris had a call from Steve Edmunds. The call came late one evening.

"Hello, Chris. It's Steve. Glad I've caught you in. I'm ringing about that antique auction."

"Ah! About time. I was thinking it must be coming up soon. When is it?"

"Next Wednesday. I've seen a catalogue and most of the items from the Wilson house are coming up for sale at that auction. "

"Is the catalogue online, Steve? If it is I can access it and check it out before I come over."

"Yes, it will be online by now. If you hang on I'll get my printed copy and give you the relevant lot numbers." Steve came back to the phone and gave his friend the details, then he rang off.

Chris searched the Antique Gazette auction site, and found the catalogue, which was well illustrated. He could see photographs of all the lot numbers Steve had given him. The sale looked well worth a visit, for as well as the Wilson's stuff there were three antique barometers in need of restoration and a few interesting clocks. He was one of the few restorers still undertaking the restoration of old mercury barometers. No new mercury barometers were being produced as mercury was regarded by most of the trade as too hazardous to handle. New EU regulations had put a stop to its use. He printed off a copy of the items that interested him and put the details to one side until he had time to do some research on them.

The lacquered clock case he had bought from Steve, stood in the showroom, fully restored but waiting to be reunited with its movement and brass dial. Chris had found a fault with the escape wheel in the eight-day movement and had contacted a specialist clock maker to cut him another one. When the new wheel arrived by post it had to be fitted onto the original arbour and then the steel pallets on the anchor escapement were filed and adjusted to work properly. This depthing was a painstaking and time-consuming task. The new wheel was in and out of the works several times, as he tried to get a perfect fit with the anchor escapement. Finally, the job was done and the clock movement married to the dial.

When the restored movement was screwed onto the seat board, the lines and weights fitted and the pendulum attached, he stepped back to admire the clock. It certainly looked a lot better than when it arrived in his workshop. He swung the pendulum, adjusted the tick of the clock and let it run so he could regulate it. Even old grandfather clocks, like that one, could be regulated to indicate the time accurately; certainly, within a minute a week. He was pleased to find everything worked fine. He stood the finished clock in the window of his showroom, wound up the weights, set it to the correct time and set the pendulum in motion. He stood and listened to the satisfying sound of the clock ticking properly with a perfect beat.

The bell on the lacquer clock was original but it was much smaller than the usual grandfather clock bell. It had a nice, high-pitched ring to it and complimented the clock perfectly. He was standing at the back of the display window listening to the sound of the clock, checking it was in tick and striking the correct hours, when a car drew up outside. A smartly dressed, middle aged, woman got out of the vehicle and came into the shop.

Chris' heart sank when he recognised Veronica Gibbs, the woman who had taken delivery of an Art Nouveau cabinet at her home in Uppingham and had been sunbathing in her garden in the nude!

"Hi" She smiled at him. "I thought I would come and visit you at your shop." She had a summer dress on with a low neckline, which she occasionally tugged down to better show off her ample cleavage. The hint wasn't lost on him. He tried to be civil and smiled back at her but he studiously avoided any glances in the direction of her chest!

She pushed herself up against him and pursed her lips. "You're not shy are you Christopher?"

"No of course not." He stepped back to give her the message he wasn't interested, but he didn't want to upset a good paying customer.

She moved closer again. She smelled of some heavy perfume and had ladled it on by the overpowering odour of it. He was finding the situation embarrassing and was considering how to end it without upsetting her, when the door opened and the Reverend John Smyth came into the shop. He quickly disengaged himself from Mrs Gibbs and went over to greet him. "I'm glad to see you, vicar."

John looked over at the lady visitor and spoke to the dealer. "I'm sorry if I interrupted you dealing with a customer. Shall I call back?"

"No, no, John!" Chris was perhaps a bit too eager to beg the vicar to stay.

John's grin widened and he looked over at Mrs Gibbs questioningly.

Veronica, realising she was not able to continue with her seduction, walked to the door. "Sorry we can't do business, Christopher. Maybe some other time?"

The dealer nodded, but his face must have told her the answer was a definite no. When she had left the shop, he turned to John. "Thank goodness you turned up when you did."

The vicar laughed out loud. "I know all about Mrs Veronica Gibbs. I occasionally stand in at the Uppingham church services and I've heard quite a bit about her. One husband doesn't seem to be enough for that lady."

Chris shook his head. "I think I'd better arrange for you to be here every time she calls. Now, what can I do for you? Have you come to collect the writing slope? I have completed the restoration. I was going to ring you later today."

"I dropped in on the off chance you had some new

antique Oak carvings but I'm thrilled that you ve had time to restore my writing slope. I write a lot of letters by hand and that slope sits on my knee just right. I can't be bothered with these new-fangled laptop computers. I think a hand-written letter is far more personal."

Chris fetched the writing slope from his workshop and placed it on a side table in the shop so that John could check it.

"Wonderful. You wouldn't know it had been damaged. What do I owe you for it?"

"That I can't say. I haven't had time to price the job. I'll let you know when I've worked it out."

"I'm glad I called. I never expected you to have done the box so quickly. Tell me, anything new in stock, since I was last here?"

"There's only the lacquered clock in the window, but I know your ceilings at the cottage are far too low for it. I did restore a Vienna regulator recently."

John nodded, but wall clocks didn't interest him. He moved towards the door. "Well, I must be off. I have a christening over at the church in fifteen minutes. Just thought I'd call in case you'd come by anything new."

"Thanks for rescuing me. You arrived very timely."

The vicar grinned impishly as he made to leave then he turned and said "I did recognise her car you know when I saw it parked outside your shop. I just wondered if you needed any help."

Later that evening, just before closing time, Chris went down to the Barrowick Arms for a nightcap and a word with Sara. She seemed pleased to see him

"Chris! Lovely to see you. You don't usually come down

this late."

" I wanted to have a word with you, so I might as well have a pint of my usual while I'm here."

Sara pulled him a pint of best bitter and placed it on the bar. "Well? What's on your mind?"

"That sale over in Norfolk. It's next Wednesday. That's your day off, I believe. Are you still interested in coming with me?"

"Oh yes! I've never been to an antique sale and I would love to experience one properly and not just watch it on the telly. I'll arrange it with mum."

He laughed. When you had been to as many sales as he had, and wasted months of his life waiting for items to come up, there was little to be excited about. "OK. Let me know if you definitely intend to come. It will be a very early start as the sale will start at 10 o'clock in the morning and there's no point in not viewing the goods first."

Sara seemed delighted with the offer. He only hoped she wouldn't be too disappointed with her first antique sale. It may look glamorous on TV but it had its drawbacks. It could be a tiring and frustrating day waiting for lots to come up for sale then being outbid for them. On some occasions, the items did not live up to the online photographs or the auctioneer's written description of them.

## Chapter Eleven

On the morning of the Norfolk sale, Chris woke up early. He'd set his alarm for 6am. He telephoned the pub to check that Sara was about and getting ready to go with him. It was a dull morning and had started to rain but the forecast for East Anglia was good and he was hopeful of a better day at the sale.

At 6.30am he picked up Sara from the Barrowick Arms and drove the van through Lincolnshire and on to Norfolk. They had arranged to meet Steve Edmunds at the sale so they went straight to the saleroom. Steve's battered old station waggon wasn't difficult to spot, so he parked next to it and walked into the saleroom at about half past nine; just half an hour before the sale was due to start. That thirty minutes gave him time to view the items being offered and to make his mind up to bid for them or to leave them alone. They found Steve viewing the furniture. The saleroom was already getting busy with punters and antique dealers checking the offering.

"Hello!" Steve seemed genuinely pleased they'd made it. He was holding a walking stick in one hand and the back of a balloon backed chair in the other, checking the soundness of the joints on it. He replaced the chair, shook hands with Chris and smiled at Sara.

Chris noticed Steve's walking stick straight away. It was a nice Malacca stick with a round, white metal, top. It must have been early 19th century by the look of it. He couldn't resist a comment. "Nice cane Steve. Where did you get that one?"

"It's a bit of my stock that I bought at auction a few years ago. It's nothing special." He seemed quite dismissive and wasn't very forthcoming.

Chris took the hint and changed the subject. "Show me the stuff that came from the Wilson house. I'll start with that."

Steve walked down the rows of furniture and stopped at an antique writing bureau. "This bureau, and those over there." He pointed with his walking stick to about ten items with consecutive lot numbers.

"Right, let's take a look."

The bureau was a nice Georgian mahogany one with three drawers and a lift up top. Chris checked the drawers then looked into the interior. It was nice, not extra special, but sound and clean. Such bureaus always have a few secret drawers in them so he checked for those first. It's surprising what you sometimes find in the hidden drawers. He'd once found a bundle of old white, five-pound notes in an old bureau he'd bought at a farm sale.

This bureau had more than its fair share of secret compartments. Chris found six in all but every one was empty except for a few paperclips and old shop receipts.  He had been hoping to see some more diamonds or other valuables, but knew that was always going to be extremely unlikely.  He was just pushing the last of the secret compartments back into place when he noticed the two men who had accosted Steve at his shop in Cley. He turned his back on them and continued checking the other sale lots.

The Wilson's furniture was not of much interest to Chris but he did find, among the other lots,  a couple of fusee wall clocks that he thought he would bid for.  Punters do like the old round fusee wall clocks that used to be in every schoolroom and in all the railway station waiting rooms up and down the country. They have such a definite and reassuring tick, and they keep very good time.  The fusee was an invention used to even out the pull of the clock spring so that the power was evenly distributed over the entire week the clock was running, ensuring very good timekeeping.  Schools and railways needed accurate clocks if anywhere did. Now that electronic timepieces were available, the old fusee clocks became redundant and regularly came onto the market. Doctor Beeching brought a flood of them for sale when he closed all those stations!  Punters like the sound and the looks of the old clocks, especially in a kitchen. They have a comforting tick and are an antique with a proper use.

He checked the clocks, making sure they had their correct pendulums and checked the springs were sound, using the multi-sized clock key he always kept in his pocket. There was some work to be done on them, mainly re-bushing and cleaning but that kind of work was routine for him. Those two clocks were well worth buying,  at the right price of course.

Steve came over to him just as he put the second clock back on the table. "I see our friends are here from the other days"

"Yes, I noticed them both."

"They've got Barry Montgomery with them. He's the ex-copper who came to your shop looking for a writing slope." Steve nodded in the men's direction.

Chris glanced across the room. Sure enough, it was the man with the scar on his chin and he was deep in conversation with the two who accosted Steve in Cley.

"Looks like they are still searching through Wilson's belongings. I wonder what they're hoping to find." He winked knowingly at Steve.

Just then four men marched into the room and started looking through the lots. From their demeanour and the expert way they quickly checked each piece of antique furniture, homing in on the weak points of table legs and chair joints, Chris knew they must be in the trade.

Steve tapped him on the shoulder. "That's bad. That lot are members of our local trade who usually work in a ring. I don't think we'll get a lot of bargains here today."

Chris looked at Steve and frowned. The Ring was a term used for a group of dealers who work together to outbid other buyers and get bargains by not bidding against each other. They share the expenses and auction the lots amongst themselves, after the sale has ended. The practise had been outlawed some time ago. It was illegal to artificially keep a price down like that, but there's little that can really be done about a group working the saleroom like that.

Chris turned and walked to his van with Sara at his side. All seemed normal and quiet. Most of the punters had left the saleroom and the car park was emptying fast but when he went to get into the van he found the three men who had bought the bureau were waiting for him and they were barring his way.

The skinny man, the one who had been talking to Steve outside his shop in Cley, spoke first. "What did you find in that bureau then?"

Chris shook his head and frowned. They must have seen him check the bureau, or the porter had told them he had searched it thoroughly. He answered truthfully. "Nothing but dust and cobwebs." Suddenly he heard Sara scream behind him. He turned quickly to see Barry Montgomery had grabbed her by the wrists. Chris was about to run over to punch him when the heavy stepped in between them.

The dealer glared at him. "Didn't I teach you enough of a lesson last time we met?"

The man sneered, put his hand into his pocket and pulled out a knife. Chris saw the steel blade glint in the sunlight. This was getting too dangerous; three against one, they had hold of Sara, and now they had a weapon. This was serious. He eyed the opposition and was about to launch myself onto the large bloke when Steve appeared from around the back of the van.

In one swift movement Steve twisted the handle of his walking stick and pulled out a long thin steel blade. Before it really registered with Chris that Steve had brought a sword-stick with him, his mate lunged at the man holding the knife and thrust the narrow blade deep into his thigh.

101

The heavy let out a scream, dropped his knife and fell to the ground clutching his leg. A dark, blood stain, spread across his trousers as he lay squirming in pain. The other two men stopped what they were doing when they heard their mate's cry. Steve turned to face them the sword still in his hand. They let go of Sara and ran.

Steve shouted after them "No good running away. Your mate here needs a lift to hospital before he bleeds to death."

The wounded man got up from the ground and limped after his companions.

Chris turned to Steve. "Thanks mate. That was timely."

Before Steve could answer, Sara burst into tears. Chris ran over to her and put his arms around her. "Are you hurt? Are you OK?"

"I'm fine." She wiped her eyes. "It's the shock. I'm OK...I'm OK... but my brooch is broken." She pointed to the silver brooch, which was lying on the ground, trodden into the soil and looking a very sorry sight.

Chris picked up the Georg Jensen silver bird, rubbed the dirt off it and inspected it. It had indeed been damaged. The pin and fixing on the back of it were squashed flat and the polished surface was scratched. Someone had put a boot on it in the struggle. "I am so sorry Sara. But as long as you are alright we can do something about the brooch. I will get it repaired for you and I know just the person to do it." He prayed that Tania Wilkes could do the job.

Steve slid his blade back into his walking stick and bent down to pick up the knife that had been dropped by their assailant. He hesitated, took out his handkerchief and picked it up in that. He grinned up at them. You never know. His

102

fingerprints might prove useful to me if they try to make anything of the attack."

Chris understood exactly what he meant. Barry Montgomery, being an ex-copper, might just report Steve for using a swordstick. It is illegal to carry such a weapon in public in this country. "You've got Sara and me as witnesses, Steve. I don't think you'll have any trouble, but thanks again for your help."

Steve nodded. "Just like old times. Just returning a favour. I had a feeling that lot would be at the saleroom and I intended to be prepared for them."

"Did you know they were waiting for us?"

"No, but I knew they might try something. They are not going to let this business go, are they."

"No. I suppose not. You be careful, Steve. That's the second time you've been involved with them and that's the second time they've come off worse. Your luck may not hold for a third time. Watch your back my old mate."

Sara and Chris got into the van and drove back towards home. She was silent most of the journey. It was a shame that the skirmish had spoiled her first saleroom experience. Chris kept glancing over at her and smiling, trying to reassure her.

As they neared Barrowick he decided to make a detour and call on Tania Wilkes in Uppingham. He felt the least he could do was try to get the brooch repaired. He explained the change of plan to Sara. "I'm going to drop your brooch off at a jewelry maker's workshop. Tania Wilkes is an old friend and very experienced. She will restore the brooch if it's at all possible."

When they arrived at Tania's place he took Sara and the damaged brooch into the house to ask if it could be repaired.

"Yes." Tania was positive about it. "I can do that. It won't take long. It's just bent and needs a surface polish to get rid of the scratches. It's a popular design of Georg Jensen's, one of my favourites. Do you want to leave it with me or are you in a hurry for it?" Chris couldn't help notice that as she spoke to him she kept glancing at Sara. He could tell she was curious about their relationship and decided to introduce the girls properly to each other.

"Sara this is Tania. She makes and repairs jewelry and we often do business. I sometimes bid at auction on her behalf."

Sara smiled politely.

He turned to Tania. "This is Sara. She runs the Barrowick Arms with her mother. We've been to an auction today and we bought the Jensen brooch for her. Unfortunately, it's had a little accident."

"Ah! The Barrowick Arms. I knew I'd seen you somewhere before. Aren't you a folk singer as well?"

Sara smiled. She was pleased to be recognised for her singing.

Tania looked at Chris. He could see she was dying to ask if Sara and he were an item, but she resisted the temptation. Instead she took him completely by surprise by asking if he'd managed to sell his diamonds!

"Have you sold those valuable diamonds yet? They were cracking stones. I wondered what you actually got for them."

Chris could tell Sara was curious about this question by

the quick look she gave him, but he passed it off by mumbling that he hadn't had time. That question was embarrassing, as he had deliberately not involved Sara in the business of the precious stones. He ignored her questioning look and quickly changed the subject.

"Any chance of you doing the brooch now, Tania? Sara is dying to wear it."

Tania took the brooch to her workbench and straightened the back pin. She then polished the front of the silver on a buffing wheel using jeweller's rouge. It took her just a few minutes to finish the job. She rubbed the brooch with a soft cloth to remove the last traces of the red abrasive and handed it back to Chris. "There. All done. You'd better pin it on your friend to see how it looks." Tania brought over a mirror for Sara to see her work in place.

He pinned the brooch onto Sara's top and held up the mirror for her to see. She seemed delighted with the result.

"That is a classic piece of modern jewelry." Tania said. "Georg Jensen is one of the best silver smiths of the 20th century and his work is very collectable. Look after it and it will increase in value as the years go by."

Sara grinned appreciatively. She looked in the mirror and toyed with her new acquisition, moving it from side to side to get the best effect.

"What do I owe you?" Chris asked.

"Nothing, as it's for you. It didn't take me a minute to sort out. Anyway, I have my eye on some costume jewelry coming up for sale at the Oakham saleroom. I know you'll be going as it's an antique sale. If I ring you and let you know the catalogue numbers maybe you could bid for them for me?"

"Any time, Tania. You know I will willingly help you out."

When we got back into the van, Sara was very quiet.

"You OK?" He asked.

"Tania seemed very interested in me and very familiar with you. Is she another of your women? "

Chris nearly choked, 'another of his women?' That comment was totally unexpected! But when he considered the situation he understood where she was coming from with that question. After all, they had seen Vickie, his ex, in Norfolk and that must have reminded Sara of a previous unfortunate occasion when Vickie had visited his shop to try to get back with him after their divorce. Unfortunately, when Vickie had decided to strip off her clothes at his flat and walk downstairs to the workshop naked to try to remind him of their married days, Sara had walked in on the scene.

He reassured her. "No. Don't be daft. I have a good business arrangement with Tania and nothing else. And she has done an excellent job on your brooch."

"What was she on about diamonds being sold? She seems to know a lot about your business dealings. "

He had been half expecting that question and had decided the least Sara knew about the diamonds, the better it would be. "Oh that! I bought a small diamond brooch, ages ago. It was damaged but the stones were OK. I must get around to selling them sometime to cover my costs. "

Sara fell silent and appeared to be satisfied with that explanation.

When they got back to Barrowick, Chris dropped Sara off at her home and went to his flat to freshen up. He had already told her he intended to call back at the pub for a meal as soon as he'd tidied himself. He had a leisurely shower and got changed. When he did eventually make it to the pub, Sara was already busy behind the bar helping her mother. She was still wearing the silver brooch and kept fingering it to check it was still attached to her top.

"Your usual?" She shouted over the heads of a group standing in front of him at the bar.

"Please. A pint of bitter and a ham sandwich or two, if you have any left."

Sara grinned and lifted a plate of ham sandwiches from under the counter.

"You know me too well!" He shook his head in mock surprise.

When the bar became quieter, Sara came over and sat beside him at his table.

He asked her "Are you alright now?" He was concerned about her after the fight in the saleroom car par. It had been a stressful day for both of them.

"I'm fine. I was just a bit shocked at the time. Your friend Steve does seem to lead an exciting life. He keeps very dodgy company. What was that all about?"

Chris chose his words carefully. He did not want Sara involved in the diamond business in any way. The less she knew about the matter, the better. "I'm not sure, but somehow Steve has fallen foul of a gang of crooks that frequent his part of Norfolk. You'll recall two of those guys were arguing with him the last time we were over that way. I do worry about him and his wife."

Sara frowned. "You were in the Paras with Steve weren't

you?"

"Yes. We were buddies in Iraq when the allies invaded there. We go back a long way."

Sara nodded but didn't ask any further personal questions, which was a relief to him. She changed the subject. "How much am I in your debt for the brooch." She fingered the little silver bird again.

"You are not in my debt at all, Sara. I would like to buy you the brooch as a thank you for a nice day out. I know we had a bit of a problem, but most of the time it was lovely and it was a pleasure to be with you. Have the brooch as a token of my thanks and as some small recompense for the unfortunate incident in the car park."

Sara was thrilled with the gift. From the way she smiled he realised he couldn't have chosen a better one

"Thanks, Chris. I do appreciate that." She bent over and kissed him on the cheek. He could only hope that gesture had put her mind at rest about other women because he was quite happy with their arrangement. After his messy divorce from Vickie, he did not want too many complications in his life. His relaxed friendship with Sara was just what he needed.

Shortly after that exchange, she had to go and help her mother with another group of customers who had just walked into the bar. Chris finished his snack and ordered another pint of bitter. It had been a long and tiring day. He had not really bought enough stock to cover his costs but at least Sara had enjoyed herself at her first antique auction. He was glad he had decided to present Sara with the Georg Jensen brooch as a gift. She had been welcome company. She deserved some compensation for the rough handling she had experienced.

108

## Chapter Thirteen.

At the weekend, Chris was contacted by the auction house near the Birmingham jewelry quarter, where he had enquired about selling his diamonds. They had a sale of precious stones planned and could include his lot. He arranged to deliver the stones to them on the Wednesday morning. He telephoned Steve and advised him to send his stones back to him by tracked post so they could be included in the same sale. Two days later he received the diamonds he had given to Steve to add to his own. He took all the stones and drove over to the West Midlands where the auctioneer checked them all.

"Nice stones Mr Doughty. What did you want to do? Do you want me to value them and put a reserve on them or are you willing to let them find their own level at auction? "

From past experience, Chris always put a reserve on things he wanted to sell at auction, that way the item would not be sold at a price too low for him to accept. It doesn't often happen, but occasionally there is little interest in an auction lot and someone gets a real bargain. Unfortunately, the seller is disappointed and loses out. He was not averse to getting things cheaply for himself but he did want a proper return on anything he offered for sale. The auctioneer finished valuing the stones.

"Clear stones, good colour and no inclusions." He checked the carat weight of each stone and made a note of it. "These should sell to the trade for a good sum." He wrote down his valuation and showed it to his customer. The figure was no surprise to Chris as it was very similar to the valuation Tania Wilkes had suggested, but it pleased him to see it in writing from an expert.

"Would you recommend I sold them as one lot or should I split them into smaller lots?" Because of the high value of the diamonds, Chris favoured splitting them into smaller lots but he was willing to be guided by the auctioneer.

"That's up to you, Sir."

"Right. I would like to split them into four lots."

Chris put the stones he had given Steve to one side as one lot then divided the others into three smaller parcels. "That should do it."

The auctioneer agreed. "Good idea. Maybe some of the smaller jewelry makers might go for two or three of these stones in a single lot as they will be an expensive buy. Not everyone can afford a bulk buy."

Chris got a receipt for the diamonds then went into Birmingham city centre to do some shopping. He needed a new pair of shoes and Barrowick didn't cater for such items. He shopped in the Bullring and found just what he wanted.

After buying his shoes, he found a small back street coffee bar and enjoyed a drink and a sandwich before he drove back to Rutland.

On the way home, he received a call on his mobile from Steve. He ignored the call as he was driving on the motorway and he intended to phone him later anyway to let him know what was happening about the diamonds. Chris was sure Steve would be glad to get the money from the sale as his antique business seemed to be going through a difficult patch.

Back in Barrowick, he called at the pub for another bite to eat and to have a chat with Sara. It was mid-afternoon and too late for a set lunch but Sara managed to rustle up some sandwiches for him as usual.

She was pleased to see him. "I can do cheese and pickle if that suits you?"

"That's fine, Sara. I've been busy and haven't had time to stop and eat properly."

Sara pulled him a pint of bitter and leaned on the bar to talk as she dried some newly washed beer glasses and stacked them beneath the counter. The pub was practically empty except for two fishermen who were talking quietly over their beers at a corner table.

She took him up on his remark. "Busy? Where have you been today? Anywhere interesting?"

"Actually, I've been to Birmingham to an auction house." He didn't expand on his business there.

"Buy anything interesting?"

"No. But I did go into the centre and bought myself a decent pair of shoes."

"Last of the big spenders!"

He grinned. Sara knew him well enough to know that he rarely spent any money on himself. "I had no choice, Sara. My toes where sticking out of the end of my old shoes!" She batted him on the head with her tea cloth and burst out laughing.

When he got home and had dealt with the day's post, he decided to return Steve's phone call.

"Steve. You called me. Sorry I didn't take the call. I was on the motorway at the time."

"That's OK. I guessed you must have been busy."

He could tell from Steve's voice, he was not happy. "What's happened Steve? You don't sound very pleased with yourself."

"We had another incident last night."

"Oh dear! What happened?"

"Someone threw a brick through the shop window in the early hours of this morning."

"Oh dear! Any ideas who?"

"It was someone on a motorbike. I heard them rev up and scorch off towards Cromer."

"Any clue who might have it in for you?"

"No, nothing solid, but I suspect it's the same gang who accosted you at the local auction. The people who want their diamonds back."

Chris fell silent while he considered this comment. He was almost sure Steve was right. Finally, he said. "I have taken the diamonds to Birmingham where they will value them and auction them next week. At least you will have the satisfaction of getting your money for them. You can pay for a new window with it and have a lot left over."

"Oh that's no problem. We are insured, but I suppose the premiums will go up after this."

"Did you report it to the police?"

"Yes, but they really haven't a clue. There are no surveillance cameras in this sleepy village and I doubt anyone was about to witness the attack at that time of the morning. We don't usually get vandalism around here so they have no one in the frame for it. They gave me a an incident number but I guess it will just add to the local unsolved crime figures."

Chris didn't really know what to advise Steve. He knew he was quite capable of looking after himself, as he had with his swordstick at the Norfolk auction, but there was little he could do about wanton damage to his business. What could you do to stop a brick being thrown through your window in the middle of the night?

"I'm sure they will give up when they realise you can't help them, Steve. Anyway, if you need me I will come straight over. We two can handle those yobs if we need to. If necessary we can contact a few old mates from the Paras. Keep your pecker up and give my regards to Dawn."

"I will, but funny you should mention the Paras. We have a group locally of ex Paras who meet in Norwich. Just an informal crowd of the lads who get together for a drink and a natter a few times a year. We have a meet coming up in two weeks' time. I'll put out feelers to a few close mates."

"Sounds good. Anybody I would know among them?"

"Johnny Stevens and his brother are in the gang. You'll remember them."

"Ah! Mad Johnny. Give him my regards. Last time I saw him, he was being marched off between two burley military policemen and put on a charge. On that occasion he was due for the glasshouse, that's for sure. What's he doing these days?"

"When I last spoke to him he was running a scuba diving school. He's into diving on shipwrecks. Thinks he'll make his fortune from sunken treasure."

"Are there many treasure ships sunk off the Norfolk coast?"

"Search me? You''ll have to ask him."

After that conversation Chris made himself a coffee and sat in his favourite chair by the French windows overlooking Rutland Water thinking over recent events. If only Dawn hadn't blurted out the fact that her husband had some diamonds. Sometimes an innocent remark to a friend can set unexpected events in motion. If only she'd kept quiet. But he knew it was no good worrying about things that he couldn't alter. Steve and he would have to brazen this one out. The peaceful scene on Rutland Water; the fishing' boats drifting over the smooth surface and water birds feeding in the shallows, had a calming effect on him. He could only hope he had heard the last of the Norfolk gang.

## Chapter Fourteen

The day after his visit to the West Midlands auction house, Chris planned to spend time in his workshop catching up on several small restoration jobs that he had been ignoring. He had been absent from his shop a lot lately, what with deliveries to customers, going to auctions and the trip to Birmingham. There were several gilt picture frames waiting to be repaired. He decided to start on those.

Damaged swept gold picture frames could be bought for silly money at auction because few people wanted to restore them; even fewer had the time and the skill, so he always bid for them and bought them if they were cheap enough. Good frames would always sell to local artists wanting an expensive looking surround for their work, and he occasionally picked up old oil paintings and watercolours in house clearance sales and needed a frame to complete them before he displayed them in his shop. He started to take some plasticine impressions of the missing plaster parts he needed to reproduce and was engrossed in that task when the shop bell sounded, heralding a punter. He wiped his hands, took off his soiled apron and went into the sales area.

The newcomer turned to face him "Hello. I bet you're glad to see me."

The dealer was taken aback. It was Veronica Gibbs, the naked lady! "What can I do for you, Mrs Gibbs?" Chris pointedly emphasised the 'Mrs' in that question.

"That depends, dear. I am looking for some more Art Nouveau pieces. I am redecorating our guest room and would love to do it up in that style."

He shrugged his shoulders. "I've nothing like that for sale at the moment. Tell you what, I'll make a note in my diary to look out for things at the next sales I attend."

"Wonderful." She sidled up to him, stood very close and smiled. He could smell that same awful heavy perfume she seemed to favour. She had a low-cut blouse with a large paste brooch at her cleavage. He was well aware the jewelry was fake but he took a step back and alluded to it to change the subject.

"I do like your diamond brooch, Mrs Gibbs. That must be worth a small fortune."

She giggled and fingered the brooch. "Silly boy, these are just Swarovski crystal, not diamonds at all. My husband bought it for me. Even he wouldn't spend a fortune on diamonds for me."

Chris apologised and turned to go back to his workshop. "Must go, Mrs Gibbs. I left a glue pot on the gas ring. Left unattended it could boil over and damage my stock. It might even burn the shop down." Veronica grimaced and shook her head but she seemed resigned to being rejected yet again.

116

"I will keep calling until you satisfy my requirements, you know."

He raised his eyebrows. Satisfying her was the last thing he intended doing. He doubted any one man was capable of such a feat!

She must have read his expression. "Silly boy. I mean until you have some more Art Nouveau for me...but I'm sure I could satisfy you in other ways, if you'd let me." With that parting promise she left the shop.

The dealer sighed with relief. After Veronica had departed he took a break from work and made himself a coffee. The conversation about her crystal brooch had given him an idea. He would have to find out where he could get his hands on some of those crystals.

A few days after this conversation with Mrs Gibbs, Chris attended the antique sale that Tania Wilkes had mentioned. He bid on her behalf for the antique jewelry she wanted and managed to get most of it. Tania knew her stuff and had set realistic prices for the items. He also managed to buy a wall mirror that needed a bit of attention but was the right price for him to sell at a profit. Maybe that would keep Mrs Gibbs quiet for a time? He doubted it would keep her happy, but it might just keep her temporarily quiet!

After lunch he took the jewelry over to Uppingham to Tania's home where she had her workshop.

Tania stopped working at her bench and stood up to greet him. "Hello Chris. Good to see you again."

"I managed to get most of the jewelry you wanted at auction. I got it cheap. Only the diamond engagement ring made more than you were prepared to pay."

"Marvellous. You really are a pal, Chris. Now lets see the goods and let me know what I owe you."

She checked the items then wrote him a cheque to cover the cost. "I feel a bit guilty bringing you out here to Uppingham just to suit me. Is there anything I can do for you?"

"You can tell me about Swarovski crystals. What are they, and are they expensive? "

"Not really. It depends on the size and colour. They are man-made from various metals and glass. The ones produced by the Swarovski factory are considered the best artificial stones for costume jewelry. I use some similar ones, but a less expensive sort, in my costume jewelry making. Do you want some?"

"I need a few small ones. Just plane glass coloured ones will do."

Tania went over to a cabinet by her workbench and took out several containers. "Here, take a look at these." She poured some cut-glass crystals onto the bench. "Any of these, suit you?"

The dealer looked at the collection of glistening stones and picked out about a dozen of the smaller ones. "These will do me fine. How much do I owe you?"

She smiled. "Nothing; You owe me nothing. Take the crystals as a thank you for bidding for me and bringing me the antique jewelry. I still think I'm getting the best of the bargain."

She put the crystals in a twist of tissue paper and handed them to him. Chris put them into his wallet.

Tania was curious    "What are the crystals for? If you

118

need to repair a piece of costume jewelry, I would do it for you for nothing. I must be in your deb⸱ for all the auctions you attend on my behalf."

The dealer shook his head. 'I would be at the sales anyway, so it's no problem to bid for you."

Tania didn't drop the subject. "I suppose you want the stones to make good that brooch you've took the diamonds out of?"

It took him a second to recall what he had told her about the diamonds he'd found in the writing slope. "...er... Yes. The diamond brooch... It seems a shame not to use the body of it and get some money back on it. I'll superglue some of these stones in place and put it into an auction."

Tania wasn't entirely happy at the thought of him gluing in the crystals. She shook her head and frowned at him. "Well, I have offered to do the job for you."

"Thanks, but it's not that important."

She changed the subject abruptly. "Have you time for a coffee?" She didn't wait for his answer and switched on the percolator as she spoke.

"Love one. I'm in no rush to get back to work. I'm only restoring some damaged gilt picture frames and a mirror."

Tania sat on her stool beside her workbench and chatted about business as they drank the coffee. Finally, she changed the subject. "How's your pretty barmaid friend?"

"Sara? She's fine. She was thrilled with that Georg Jensen brooch repair you did for her."

"Lucky girl having a boyfriend like you to buy her presents like that...I presume you did buy it for her?"

He nodded agreement, then corrected her. "Sara is not

my girlfriend we are just good friends," Which was true, as Sara and he were both busy people and had deliberately kept their friendship on a relaxed basis.

Tania took him completely by surprise with her next remark. "I could do with a man friend like you." She smiled and looked down at her hands, avoiding looking directly at him.

He got the message. It struck him then how perceptive Sara had been when they called to get the Jensen brooch repaired. When they'd left Tania's studio Sara had asked him outright if Tania was another of his women! Females seemed to be attuned to those undercurrents, far more than he ever was.

He drained the last of his coffee and put the mug on the bench. "I must be off now, Tania. Thanks for the coffee and the crystals. Glad I could help with the auction lots."

She saw him out to his van and waved him off.

Back home he put the cut glass crystals on a plate and picked out ten of them that more or less matched the size of the diamonds he was selling in Birmingham. He had an idea he could pass them off to the Norfolk gang if it came to a showdown with them. He found an old white handkerchief and cut a narrow piece from it, choosing the hem as it looked a bit like the ribbon that had contained the diamonds. He stitched the crystals into the ribbon and added a string tail to it, just like the hiding place of the ten valuable stones he had found in the writing slope. A rub with dust from the workbench and the ribbon looked convincing. If he could fool the late Richard Wilson's friends and they discovered for themselves that the diamonds weren't real, they might just think their colleague, Mr Wilson, had fooled them and leave Steve and him in peace. It was a long shot but well worth a try. He decided to ring Steve and set things in motion.

"Steve. It's Chris. Bad news I'm afraid."

"Oh! What's the problem, mate?"

"Those diamonds, they are not cosha; they are not the real thing."

Steve listened in silence as his friend explained what had happened.

"I took them to an auctioneer in the Birmingham jewelry quarter to be valued and sold. The expert valuer rang back and told me they were fakes; very good fakes but nevertheless they are only lead glass crystals and as such of little value. They were not interested in trying to sell them for me. He's posting them back to me to save me a journey."

Steve just grunted then fell silent.

Chris could feel his disappointment. "You still there, Steve?"

"Yes. What I don't understand is how your so-called expert got it so wrong? You seemed sure of their value when you originally rang me."

"I'm sorry Steve. I am as gutted as you must be. The person who gave me the original valuation is just a local jewelry designer. I don't think he has handled many diamonds before. You'll have to tell Dawn she's not as rich as she thought she was. "

Steve was really gutted. He didn't immediately answer. He could be heard sighing down the phone. It was obvious how disappointed he felt. At last he spoke.

"That's a sod! I really needed that money. Things are bad

121

enough without this disappointment."

"I know, Steve. I feel the same." Chris felt awful lying to his mate but he needed Dawn to blab to her friends about her disappointment in the hope the news would get back to Wilson's associates. Maybe that would get them off their backs and he could surprise Steve with the truth when things had calmed down.

Nothing more was said. The Cley dealer rang off, full of disappointment. Chris wasn't too pleased with the deception but he had done what he set out to do. Sometimes you had to be tough for the common good; sometimes the means did justify the ends. That was good tactics, in the army and still applied now he was in civvy street

## Chapter Fifteen.

The next morning Chris had a phone call from the Oakham police. The Northampton police force had traced the stolen clock back to an antique runner from their area. When they contacted the dealer who had sold the bracket clock to him, he had told them where he had obtained it. The clock had been bought from one of his local contacts who acted as a runner, buying privately and selling to the trade from the back of his car. The police had taken the runner into custody and charged him with the theft of the clock. He was due to go for trial the very next week.

Chris was called as a witness for the prosecution and had to attend the Crown Court at Northampton. The dealer wasn't pleased with the interruption to his business but he knew he had little choice but to attend the trial. He was a little curious about Crown Court trials anyway and he knew he could make a claim for the travelling expenses and his loss of earnings. He decided to try and enjoy the experience and make the best of it.

On the morning of the trial he turned up and signed in at the Crown Court. The waiting room was very busy with bewigged and black gowned barristers coming and going, and police officers milling around. Eventually the accused was escorted into the room. He was a weedy looking lad of about twenty years of age. He looked very worried and downtrodden. Chris felt sorry for him.

The court officials started the proceedings by parading the possible jurors in front of the accused and his solicitor. Chris watched with interest as each juror was checked and either accepted or rejected by the defendant. The choice seemed rather arbitrary but he did hear that one of the jurors, an elderly man, had been the accused's maths teacher at school. The lad must have had bad memories of that man and wouldn't accept him on the jury; or maybe he just wasn't good at maths!

Chris sat in the waiting area until he was called to give evidence. When at last he was called, he was escorted to a booth in the courtroom where he stood facing the jury and the Judge. He found the experience fascinating, never having attended a Crown Court before.

The Judge was a portly, middle aged, man wearing a judicial wig and a dark gown. He sat slouched at his desk, seemingly inert but listening intently to the proceedings, making occasional notes and toying with his pen. The jurors sat to the left of the judge's bench, facing the witness across the courtroom. They looked to be a mixed bunch of people of various ages and backgrounds. It was the first time Chris had been involved in any kind of legal case. He found it very interesting.

An usher brought the bracket clock into the courtroom and placed it on a table in front of Chris. He eyed the clock and immediately recognised it as his stock. Then the prosecuting barrister started his questioning.

"You are Christopher Doughty an antique dealer from Barrowick in Rutland who was offering this clock for sale?"

"Yes."

"You have an unusual business in that you restore clocks and antiques as well as retailing them?"

"Yes."

"Tell the court what you did to this clock before offering it for sale."

Chris described the process of restoring the bracket clock, making sure the court understood he did not remove the brass plaque from it as that had been removed before he bought it. He also emphasised that the restoration of the damage caused by the removal of the name plaque had been solely to make it more saleable and not to deceive or conceal the clock's past history.

The barrister continued with that line of questioning for some time. Chris began to feel the man must be paid by the word because he was dragging out the cross-examination to great length. He also noticed some of the jurors were fidgeting in their seats, getting bored with the way the case was going. Even the judge started tapping his pen on the bench in obvious frustration. At last the judge spoke up and warned the barrister he was wasting time with his line of questioning and not getting on with the case.

"Mr Folds, you are wasting time. Get on with it!"

125

The witness smiled to himself. He couldn't have put it better himself.

The barrister changed his line of questioning. "Tell the court where and when you bought the clock."

Chris explained he had bought the item on one of his regular buying trips into Northamptonshire. "I bought it at David Brown's antique barn near Finedon. It was a regular trade stop for me." He held out the receipt and the other paperwork for the court to see.

The judge asked to see the documents, made a few notes then handed them back to the witness.

All the time this was going on, Chris couldn't help noticing the accused, who was sitting to his right, flanked by two police officers. The lad looked bored with the proceedings and didn't seem to be taking much notice.

After he had informed the court where and when he bought the clock, Chris was dismissed but he was asked to stay in the waiting area in case he was called again to explain some further facts. He went back to the waiting room and got himself a coffee from the vending machine in the corridor. He arrived back to his seat in time to hear the court usher calling for Mr David Brown, the dealer who had sold him the clock. The prosecution were trying to prove a trail leading back to the accused.

In the courtroom Brown asserted he had bought the clock from the accused, who was a regular runner in the area, picking up stock wherever he could and selling it into the trade. It was a precarious living but one seen regularly on the margins of the antique business. It was a hand to mouth way to exist and often lead to doubtful practices, like handling stolen goods.

When David Brown was dismissed from the witness stand he came into the waiting room and sat next to Chris.

"Sorry you got involved in this business, Chris. I will reimburse you for the clock. It's not fair you should lose out because of my mistake."

"That's very good of you." He was pleasantly surprised at this offer.

"You've been a regular customer for the past few years. I can't have you going short."

Chris was pleased with the man's attitude. He had always found Dave to be a fair and honest dealer. That was one of the reasons he regularly called on him for stock. It was good to be proved right in his assessment of the man. He leaned over and asked quietly. "What's going to happen to the lad in there? Do you think he'll go down?"

"I don't know. Kevin Spicer is pleading not guilty and not declaring where he bought the clock. He is saying it is more than his life is worth to split on his suppliers as he would fear for his life if he did drop them in it."

"Will it wash? Do you think that defence will save him?"

"I don't know. That's up to the jury but the police are trying to pin the actual burglary on him and he is saying he is the innocent victim of a scam, much as you and I have been."

"Doesn't sound like a strong case against him. Why do the police think he did it? Any idea?"

"Well, he has form, but not for stealing. He's been busted a few times for possession and for selling hard drugs."

"Oh! I see. So, they are pinning the burglary on him or trying to force him to reveal his source."

"That's about it."

"Interesting. I will be fascinated to see how the case ends."

While they were talking, the accused had taken the witness stand and was cross-examined at length by the prosecuting barrister. Kevin insisted he had not stolen the clock and had bought it in good faith, but no amount of questioning could elicit the name of his supplier. He kept insisted it was more than his life was worth to drop the man in it.

The defending barrister played heavily on that fact and painted a picture of a feckless youth up to his neck in trouble and mixing with the wrong people. He made a strong case of the fear his client had expressed; such a strong fear he would rather face prison than tell who his supplier had been. The jury was dismissed to go and deliberate on its verdict.

An usher came into the waiting room and approached Chris and his companion. "You are free to go now. The case is over except for the verdict."

By this time, it was early afternoon and Chris was feeling hungry. David Brown accompanied him out of the courtroom and up to the market place where he went to a cash point, withdrew £200 and repaid Chris the money he had laid out on the clock.

Chris pocketed the money and thanked the dealer. He knew David was not obliged to repay him but it was good business sense to do it. Once they had completed their business, David Brown left him in the market place and went home. Chris decided he would find a pub in the area that did bar meals and have a late lunch in Northampton. After that, he would visit a few of the local antique shops to renew acquaintances and see if he could buy anything for his stock. He felt he might as well make a day of it in Northamptonshire as he had had to come that way for the trial.

After lunch Chris visited several of the antique outlets about the city, calling on dealers he knew from the salerooms, but he managed to buy nothing that he could restore or sell. With city rates and rents to pay, the prices they were asking were too high for him. He needed to resell at a profit in an out of the way village like Barrowick, but he enjoyed talking to them, exchanging intelligence about the salerooms he had not visited and the way the business was altering. Finally, by late afternoon, he made his way back to the city centre car park where he had left his van, intending to call it a day and drive home.

At the car park, he paused in his van a few minutes drinking a can of Coke before he made for Barrowick. This delay proved fortuitous. As he sat quietly drinking, a familiar figure got out of a car parked close to him. He shrank back out of sight in his cab and watched the man pace up and down the deserted car park. The dealer had immediately recognised the newcomer as one of the Cromer gang who had attacked him at the Norfolk saleroom. There was no mistaking him. It was the slim, older one, who had accosted Steve the day Sara and he had gone to collect the lacquer clock and the writing slope. It became obvious as the man paced up and down and kept checking the time on his wristwatch, that he was waiting for someone.

After about ten minutes a young man walked into the

car park and approached the area where Chris was hidden. It was a shock for the dealer to realise it was Kevin Spicer, the lad who had been accused of stealing the bracket clock. It seemed that David Brown had predicted correctly when he thought the jury would find the accused not guilty. Here he was, a free man and walking into the town centre.

As the lad approached Chris' van, the Norfolk man walked up to him and held a quiet conversation with him. From the furtive way they kept looking around them it was obvious they were up to no good. Chris sank further out of sight in his seat and watched them. After a few minutes, conversation Kevin produce a wad of bank notes from his inside pocket and handed them over to his companion. The Cromer man went to the boot of his car and handed a small package to the lad.

Chris watched fascinated as Kevin opened the container, licked a finger and dipped it into the bag. When he pulled it out, his finger was coated with a fine white powder. He placed the finger onto his tongue and tasted it. He seemed satisfied with his purchase and nodded. The lad shook hands with his companion then walked back the way he had come, out of the car park.

Chris waited while the Norfolk man got into his car and drove out of the parking lot, then he straightened up and considered what he had just witnessed. There had been an exchange of a fair amount of money and a small package was given in return. Kevin Spicer had sampled it by tasting it. It didn't take a Sherlock Holmes to work out it was some kind of hard drug; it certainly wasn't icing sugar in that bag. Kevin was a drug addict and a pusher if David Brown had surmised correctly. Now he knew the Norfolk gang were into illegal drugs and he understood why they might have a need for the diamonds.

Diamonds are an easily portable, smal and valuable form of international currency. They are not traceable and they are acceptable as payment almost anywhere in the world. It was a safe bet the gang smuggled drugs into the country via one of the small Norfolk coastal ports and paid for them with diamonds. That would explain Richard Wilsons' unexplained wealth and the aggro Steve was now getting from the gang members.

## Chapter Sixteen

Nothing more was heard from Steve Edmunds for two whole weeks after he'd been told the disappointing news about the fake diamonds, but one afternoon after Chris returned to his workshop from a shopping expedition, he found a recorded message on his telephone. He listened to the message and was shocked by its content. He played it a second time.

"Hi Chris. This is Steve. Problems again. I had an anonymous letter this morning warning me to give back the diamonds or Dawn may have a fatal accident. I can ignore their bricks and their threats to me but Dawn's safety is a different matter. Ring me when you can."

Chris returned the call straight away. "Steve. That message sounded serious."

"Yes. I don't know what to do about it. If anything happened to Dawn, I'd never forgive myself. "

"What does she think?"

"I haven't told her. I don't know how she would react.

"I see. You're probably right. I shall have to think of a way out of this. Leave it with me and I'll get back to you as soon as I can." The dealer put down the phone and went up to his flat to make a coffee and do some serious planning. He knew he must give the fake diamonds to the Norfolk gang and hope they would accept them as the ones he had found in the writing slope. When he'd finished his coffee, he rang Steve back and suggested an answer to their problem. "Steve. I have the stones back from the Birmingham auction house. I still have the ribbon they were sewn into. I will replace the stones in the ribbon and bring them over to you. Perhaps you can arrange a meeting with that Barry Montgomery fellow, and his mates, so I can hand them over."

Steve hesitated for a few seconds then sounded very relieved. "Thanks mate. I hoped you could come up with something to sort this out. I wasn't even sure you still had the stones or if you'd disposed of them as they were worthless. I'll contact them today. When do you want to come over with the stones?"

"Any time to suit you, Steve. We can go together to meet them and hand the stuff over."

The very next morning Steve telephoned him again. "I rang Montgomery last night. He will meet us anytime you like. I told him you had only just discovered the diamonds and you would let him have them."

"Good. Ring him back. I'll be over early tomorrow morning if you can arrange a meeting at such short notice. Ring me and confirm the arrangements. Hopefully I'll see you tomorrow and this nasty business will stop."

Later that day, Steve confirmed a meeting had been set

up for mid-day the next day. The gang had insisted they met out in the open, on the pier in Cromer where they could control things.

The following morning Chris got ready for handing over the stones. He didn't trust the people he was going to meet so he took a few precautions. He put a brass knuckleduster and a pepper spray into his back pocket in case things got nasty. He placed the ribbon containing the crystals into his wallet and put that in his inside pocket. It was early in the morning, when he drove up the main street of Barrowick village, past the pub, which was in darkness as was the rest of the village, and onto the main road to Stamford. He put his foot down and drove his van into Norfolk and on to Cley.

At Steve's antique shop he found his old friend in a better frame of mind.

"You're early." Steve met him in the drive beside the shop. "I haven't told Dawn anything about this morning's meeting. I did tell her you were coming over to see some antiques in Cromer, so you know what to say to back me up on the story."

Steve had hardly voiced this explanation when Dawn came out to join them. "You've come to buy some antiques, Steve tells me. Nice to see you again."

Chris gave her a hug and went with them into the house to have a coffee.

"The customer has asked me to call after mid day." Chris explained to Dawn. "If you can spare Steve I'd like him to come with me to give me directions. He knows the area better than I do."

Dawn smiled and nodded her agreement. She was taken

in by this deception.

"Good. Well I'm early. I didn't know whether to expect a lot of traffic this way with holiday makers and caravans on the roads, but I made good time." Turning to Steve he asked. "Anything I can help you with while I'm here. Any restoration work or heavy lifting?"

"No. I have very little stock now. Money's short."

Chris shook his head. "I'm sorry mate. Maybe the tide will turn soon and you'll get some good business."

The two friends went into the house and chatted about business and old times while Dawn made them a coffee. Eventually, Chris suggested they might stretch their legs and take a stroll in the village. "I spend too much time driving these days. It's nice to have time to take a leisurely walk and see what Cley has to offer."

Steve grinned. "See what Cley has to offer? That will take about ten minutes if we dawdle!"

"All the same, I need to stretch my legs. You coming with me?"

The two men left Steve's antique shop and walked slowly along the Cromer road towards the local windmill. Cley has a wonderful example of a four sail windmill overlooking the marshes. The area is a wild life haven with wild birds living in the large reed beds surrounding the building.

"Nice windmill. Still has its four sails I see. Is it in working order?" Chris asked.

"No, not any more. It's let out as holiday accommodation but it certainly adds something to the village. It's quite a landmark. Every artist in the county has painted pictures of it at some time or another. You can buy original art work and postcards of it all over this area"

Steve abruptly changed the subject. "Now to business. We are to meet Barry Montgomery on Cromer pier, his choice not mine."

"Good. I have the stones here." Chris took the ribbon from his wallet and showed it to his companion. "I've repaired the ribbon and made sure all the stones are back in it. Hopefully that will be the end of our problems."

Steve shook his head and frowned; he was thinking of what might have been; how all his money worries could have been solved.

Chris slapped him on the back. "Don't fret, mate. I'm sure something will come along. I'll keep my eyes open and my ear to the ground to see if we can't come up with a solution to your problems." He hoped he would sell the real diamonds for a good price but he knew he'd have to keep very quiet about that until all the problems had calmed down. When he did let his friend know what was really happening, he knew he would have to swear Dawn and Steve to secrecy about their windfall.

When they got to the end of the village, they stood and looked out over the reedbeds of the bird reserve. In the distance Chris could see the shingle sea banks, which kept Cley safe from the North Sea.

"Any chance of those banks failing and the village flooding?"

Steve shook his head. "It has happened years ago. All of this area is reclaimed land. If you go further towards Holt you'll pass the old church and the large green in front of it. In the Middle Ages that area was the harbour, so you can see how far the sea has been pushed back."

"Let's hope it doesn't return and you don't get wet!"

The two friends turned and walked back into the village. Chris would have liked to continue to the sea bank but he noticed his companion was already limping badly. The old wound Steve sustained in the Paras did limit his mobility. Part way along the main road Steve stopped and leaned heavily on his walking stick. "Sorry. I can't rush these days. My back injury won't let me!"

"Don't fret. I know you got that wound in battle. You shouldn't make excuses. You are a hero."

Steve shook his head and looked for something else to say to change the subject. He pointed to the building beside them "That's the old Fishmonger's Arms where Henry Pashley used to live."

Chris frowned. "Who's Henry Pashley?"

Steve smiled, pleased to be better informed than his successful friend. "Pashley was a naturalist and taxidermist. He won a gold medal for the best specimen of a Turnstone in flight. That medal was awarded by Lord Lilford in 1880."

"Ah!. Lord Lilford of Lilford Hall. That's not far from me in Northants. He was a famous ornithologist. I've heard of him."

"Yes. Taxidermy specimens set up by Pashley, occasionally come up for auction in this area. He's well known and they fetch good prices."

"Have you ever handled any of them?"

"No, but I did sell a copy of Pashley's book, Notes on the Birds of Cley, Norfolk. And it made a good price." Steve

137

straightened up and started walking again. Soon they arrived back at his shop. Later that morning, Chris drove his friend to Cromer. They parked the van then walked slowly to the pier.

Cromer pier is still in good condition in spite of its age; the present structure was built in 1902 but it is was just the latest example of a pier built there since the middle ages. Like so many seaside piers, Cromer's has a long promenade and a theatre overlooking the sea at the end of the walk. Children fish from the sides of it for Dabs and Crabs, making it a popular holiday attraction.

When Steve got out of his van he noticed his companion had brought a walking stick with him. This was no surprise as Steve wasn't walking well, but the stick did look similar to the swordstick that he had used at the local saleroom when they were attacked. Closer inspection assured Chris it was just an ordinary cane, which his friend needed to help him walk any appreciable distance.

"I thought for a minute you'd come armed again?" Chris pointed to the walking stick.

Steve grinned. "No not this time. I don't see why we should expect trouble as they are getting what they are after."

Chris patted his back pocket to reassure himself he had the knuckleduster and pepper spray ready, in case they were needed. He wasn't as convinced as his companion that they wouldn't meet trouble.

On the pier, about half way down the wooden walk, they saw Barry Montgomery and a couple of other men waiting for them.

"Looks like they're keen to get their diamonds back." Chris said in a low voice.

Once they were closer to the men they recognised all three of them. The ex-copper had brought the thick set heavy, who had fallen foul of the sword stick, and the thin man who had accosted Steve outside his shop. From the way the big man eyed Steve's walking stick he had not forgotten the last time he had tried to attack them.

"Sorry about this." Chris smiled disarmingly. "I have only just found this ribbon of stones when I was restoring some antiques I bought locally." He held out his hand to shake hands but that friendly gesture was ignored.

"Where's the goods?" Barry Montgomery got straight to the point.

Steve took the small tape from his wallet and handed it to the man. "If that's what you mean, you're welcome to it."

Montgomery felt the length of the tape, pressing the bumps it contained and counting them as he did so. He nodded and smiled. "Looks like they are all here. All ten of them." Turning to the two dealers he held out his hands in a conciliatory gesture. "Sorry for any problems we've caused you but these are our property and we meant to get them back."

The two antique dealers said no more. They just turned and walked back towards the van. Chris turned as he left the pier and looked back at the three men. Montgomery was already on his mobile phone and kept glancing towards them as he was speaking. He assumed he was reporting back to some other associates. He automatically patted his back pocket once again to assure himself he was ready for any unforeseen attacks if they were going to be set upon on their way back to his van.

Once out of earshot, Steve expressed his frustrations. "That money would have just about kept me afloat. Those stones were definitely not legal, I'm sure. What a bloody nuisance we've had to give then back."

Chris could do nothing but agree with this companion.

As they approached the van in the car park a police car drew up and blocked the exit. Two policemen jumped out of the vehicles and quickly approached them.

Chris stopped and smiled at the officers. "Can we help?"

"We've had a complaint that your companion is carrying a concealed weapon."

Chris looked shocked. He turned to Steve. "You got a gun with you?"

Steve just grinned. He was enjoying himself.

The officer held out his hand for the walking stick. "We believe that stick is an illegal swordstick, Sir. It's against the law to carry such weapons in a public place. We need to confiscate it, and you must accompany us to the police station."

Steve gave them his walking stick and waited for their reaction. One of the policemen tried to pull the top off the stick to un-sheath a blade. He tugged at the top with one hand and held the cane tightly in his other hand, but the silver knob just came off in his fingers revealing an ordinary lacquer cane beneath it. The office looked up, red faced and embarrassed. He apologised. "Sorry Sir. We were contacted by a member of the public and told your cane hid a concealed weapon. We had to investigate the complaint."

Chris took back the cane and pushed the silver knob back into place. He turned to Steve. "We can glue this back on when we get back to your shop." Turning to the policemen who were looking very red faced and apologetic he said. "You shouldn't take any notice of Barry Montgomery and his mates. He may be an ex copper but he's also a stupid one. You'd better make out a full report of this incident, because you'll be getting a bill from us for repairs to this valuable antique cane."

The two officers exchanged worried glances then climbed back into their patrol car. As they went Chris heard one of them say. "That bloody fool Barry is a menace with his misinformation." They drove off in a hurry, their car tyres screeching as they exited the car park.

Steve broke into peals of laughter, his shoulders shaking uncontrollably. Chris grinned broadly and helped him climb into the passenger seat of the van. They went back to Cley where Dawn had prepared a fish and chip lunch for them.

"Did you buy any stock?" She asked Chris.

"Not this time, but it has been interesting. I must say, the pier at Cromer is well worth a visit. You never know who or what you may see on there."

Steve stuffed a piece of cod into his mouth to stifle a laugh.

## Chapter Seventeen

After they had eaten lunch, Chris decided he must drive back to Barrowick but he would call on a few antique dealers on his way home. He couldn't really afford to waste an afternoon so he'd take the opportunity to do some trade.

Just outside Sutton Bridge he called on another old friend. Betty Crawford was a longstanding contact who had been very helpful to him when he first started to deal in antiques.

"Chris, how lovely to see you. Long-time no see." The elderly dealer hugged him and kissed him on his cheek. "How are things in Barrowick? Still in business there?"

"Still hanging on."

"You did right to get rid of that Vickie. You know, I never did like the girl."

He grinned. Many of his friends had voiced the same opinion once he and his wife had divorced. Funny how no one had mentioned it earlier when they were still together. "I suppose you see Vickie this way occasionally now she's in business in Norwich?"

142

"No. She knows I can't stand her. She knows better than waste her time calling here. She did try it once but I saw her off with a flea in her ear."

He grinned even more then changed the subject. 'Now then, Betty, anything in stock that might interest me? You know what I usually buy; good class antiques that need a bit of TLC to increase their value."

She took him into her show room at the front of the house and switched on the lights. He looked around the stock and immediately spotted an Art Nouveau wall mirror. That might just suit Veronica Gibbs. It was a particularly nice example. Better than the one he'd bought at auction "How much is the mirror?"

Betty quoted him the trade price.

"I'll have it. I think I know just the home for it. Have you anything else that would suit me? Any damaged stock in need of restoration?"

"Come out to the barn at the back. I keep damaged goods out there for restorers like you."

Chris had hoped Betty would have something for him. She had been in business for decades in that same area and was well known in the district as far afield as Spalding and Wisbech. She was often approached to do house clearances and didn't usually buy at auction, so her prices could be reasonable as she hadn't had to bid against the ring for her goods or pay the auction fees.

"Here, take a look around. I have a lot in at the moment." She switched on the lights and stood in the doorway looking around her barn. "What about that Admiral Fitzroy? That needs some TLC. It will make a good barometer once it's restored." 143

Chris pulled the barometer from under a pile of other items and held it up to scrutinise it. It was indeed a good example of an early Fitzroy. It had a decorative mahogany case with crisply carved 'C' scrolls adorning it. All the scales were intact but the main glass tube was broken and empty. The mercury had been lost ages ago and the tube would have to be replaced.

"Any good to you? I know you used to restore barometers along with your clocks when you were trading in Stamford. Do you still do them or has the EU put a stop to all that?"

"Yes. I still have some glass Mercury tubes in stock. I'm pleased the other, smaller, weather tube is intact. That one takes some replacing."

He rubbed his finger over the smaller thermometic tube, rubbing off a thick layer of dust to reveal the cloudy solution still sealed inside it. He knew from past experience that no one supplied those weather tubes and the chemicals to fill them would be difficult to get. He had found the formula for the solution when he was researching Admiral Fitzroy. The contents consisted mainly of Camphor, strong alcohol, saltpetre and ammonium chloride in aqueous solution, but those ingredients were not easy to obtain. The crystals forming in this mixture could predict the weather by the size and shape of the precipitates. Admiral Fitzroy had been a pioneer of weather predicting and had set up the first regular weather forecasts for shipping in Britain in 1854. The admiral was an interesting character, He was the captain of the Beagle when Charles Darwin visited the Galapagos Islands.

He turned to Betty. "What do you want for it? Bear in

mind, a new Mercury tube will cost me quite a bit and they are getting very difficult to buy now the EU has banned any new Mercury barometers being made."

The old lady consulted her notebook and did some quick calculations. "You can have it for a hundred, as it's you."

Chris was pleased. That gave him quite a margin of profit. As a fully restored example of a Fitzroy in a nice mahogany frame it should fetch four hundred pounds or more. "I'll have it. Any clocks among this stuff?" He waved a hand at the mountain of old stock littering the barn.

"There's an Art Nouveau pewter shelf clock here somewhere." She started to search for it.

"Tudric is it?"

"You'll be lucky! If it had been an Archibald Knox clock from Liberty's it wouldn't be out here."

He grinned. Betty knew her stuff.

"Here it is." She held up a small pewter clock with an oval green cabochon stone let into the front of the case.

Chris took it from her and inspected it. "Not Knox, but not bad. It's a copy and it's got a bit of age on it. How much." He opened the back of the clock and inspected the movement to see if the escapement was sound. "It doesn't work you know. Needs a new escapement platform."

"I know, but someone with your experience of clocks can soon put that right."

He waited while she consulted her stock book once more.

"It will have to be fifty. Any good to you?"

"OK. I'll take the two for a hundred and fifty." He continued looking over the vast amount of stock that Betty had

145

accumulated. She stood in the doorway trying to think of other items that might interest him. Finally, she spoke. "How about a polyphon? I have a table model that needs a new spring. There are twenty or so metal discs with it so you'll not be short of mechanical music to play on it, once it's in working order again."

"I haven't sold a polyphone for years. You don't see them at auction that often." He knew the early wind up, music players made good money, especially when they had plenty of metal music discs with them. "Where are you hiding that one?"

Betty walked to the far end of the barn where she had an old wardrobe she was using as a storage unit. She flung open the doors to reveal a collection of mechanical antiques. "Here you are." She took out the Polyphon and placed it on a table. "It's a German model with a single comb of notes. I reckon the case is Walnut. What do you think?"

"It's Walnut alright." Chris tried to turn the handle to wind the spring but found there was no resistance. "Springs broken." He said.

"I know, that's why it's only fifty pounds. Surely a clock man like you could repair it?"

He checked the state of the rest of the instrument. The musical comb was complete, with no teeth missing. The case was in good order with no cracks or warping. "It's a pity the spring has broken. They are very strong springs and difficult to get. You can't just put any clock spring into a Polyphon as they are never strong enough for the job."

Betty just nodded. He wasn't telling her anything she didn't already know.

146

He looked at the instrument again, weighing up the cost of restoration and the possible profit in it. "Fifty, you say?"

"As its you."

He shook hands on the deal and placed the polyphon to one side. He was sure he could locate a strong enough spring and there was always the possibility the spring was not broken but had just come detached from its drum. He looked into the wardrobe again hoping to find some other treasures.

"There's a Swiss music box in there somewhere. The works are fine but the inlaid case needs some attention."

Chris searched for the box and found it. "A good maker. It's a Nichole Freres and plays six tunes. Pity about the box. How much for it?"

Betty consulted her stock book yet again. "Got to be four hundred. It stands me a lot of money."

"Too rich for me." Chris put the music box back into the wardrobe. "I will take the mirror, the Polyphon, the Admiral Fitzroy and the pewter clock. " He gathered all four items together and left the barn.

Betty followed him up to the house. "Good. Now come back into the kitchen and tell me how things are with you. And don't be so long calling back in future."

"Coffee?" She asked, but didn't wait for an answer. She poured him a large cup of dark brown liquid from a grubby percolator that seemed to be constantly switched on.

Chris looked into his cup. "Still running on super strength coffer I see. It will rot your insides."

"My old mother used to say it coloured your bones brown, but I don't how she knew that." Betty poured herself a drink and sat at the kitchen table. "Sit down.    You're not in a hurry are you?"

"Actually I am. I'll have to get on my way when I've downed this coffee." He took out his wallet and paid Betty for the items he had purchased from her.

The old lady grimaced at the news he was in a hurry to get back on the road. She had a soft spot for Chris and had known him for years. She had been one of the first trade calls he had visited when he left the army and went into business.

"Well, if you must rush off, don't be so long calling back this way. If you like, I will hang on to any clocks and barometers that need attention and give you a ring when it's worth your while coming over."

"You'd do that for me?" He was touched. He handed her his business card with his contact number on it.

"Of course. Must look after my good customers." She stuffed the card into her apron pocket.

Chris gave her a kiss on the cheek and left her premises. He was hoping to make a few more trade calls on his way back to Barrowick, and time was getting on.

## Chapter Eighteen

When he arrived back at his shop at Barrowick, Chris checked his emails and was pleasantly surprised to see he had one from the Birmingham auction house telling him the diamonds had all sold and they had fetched a good price. He checked their invoice online and was pleased to see they owed him £50,000. The stones had fetched more than he expected. Even with the auction house charges and VAT paid, he would get that substantial amount. He sat back and whistled out loud. That was good news. Now he had to wait until the month end when the auction house would settle their account with him and send him his cheque, only then could he sort things out with Steve and Dawn.

It was while he sat finishing his coffee and checking the rest of his emails, he heard a loud knock on the shop door. He rushed down the stairs and opened the door, hoping it was a punter.

"John, come in." He was pleasantly surprised to find it was the local vicar who had bought the writing slope, and he had another man with him.

"I hope we haven't disturbed you Chris. This is my brother in law, Charlie Brent. He wants to see that longcase clock you have in the shop."

Chris ushered them into the sales area and took his visitors over to the clock.

"Ah! It's green lacquer. John tells me it's most unusual as it's reputedly made by a lady maker." Charles put on his reading glasses and peered closely at the silvered dial and the maker's name engraved on it. "Jane Cooper. Interesting. Tell me is that original?" He turned to Chris as he spoke.

"Yes, no doubt about it. The style of the engraving is dead right and the silvered plaque is the right shape."

"Is Jane Cooper listed in Bailie?" Charles was obviously knowledgeable about clocks to be familiar with Bailie, the exhaustive list of antique clock makers.

"No. But not every clock maker has made it into that reference book."

Charlie nodded. "What do you date it at?"

"By the style of the case, the silvered brass dial, and the gilded spandrels, I'd say it's about 1760. The hands are original and a correct pattern for that date as well."

Charlie reached up and fingered one of the triangular brass spandrels that decorated each corner of the square dial. He ran his fingers over the arched section. "Hermes, I see. Messenger of the gods. Does it move? Is it an automaton?"

Chris opened the decorated lacquered door and gently

150

swung the pendulum. The silvered figure of the God with his winged heels and caduceus held aloft in one hand, rocked from side to side in time with the ticking of the clock.

Charlie turned away from the clock. "Surely, female maker are very rare in the 1700s?"

"Very rare but not unique. Jane Cooper must have been a widow. Her husband would have been a member of the London Clock Company before he died. The Clock Company would have allowed her to carry on managing his workshop so his staff was not put out of work. I've tried to do some research and narrow it down to one particular Cooper family but there are several listed at that date. It could be any of them."

"I see. So, the London Clock Company was an all-male group, which is what you would expect at that period, but they were sensible enough to compromise when jobs were at stake."

Chris nodded.

"It's a pity some of our modern Trade Unions aren't as thoughtful."

John, who had been keeping quiet during this exchange, spoke up at last. "You see, Charlie, I did get it right. What do you think?"

"I like it." He turned to Chris. "What's the best price you can do on it?"

The dealer knew full well what price the clock stood him as he had taken the clock from his mate Steve to help him out and had really paid too much for it. He had also spent a lot of time doing the restoration work on it. "The lowest I can go is £1750. I need to cover my time as well as the material costs."

Charlie stroked his chin and considered the price. At last he spoke. "What about one and a half?"

Chris shook his head. "No. I'm sorry. I have quoted you my lowest price as you are a friend of John's and he is such a good customer."

Charlie relented and smiled. He held out his hand and shook on the deal. "OK. One and three quarters it is. But I will want it delivered and set up properly."

Chris readily agreed. "Where are you living?"

"Bringhurst, over in Northamptonshire. Is that OK?"

"Fine. Let's arrange a date and time and I will bring it over and set it up. Just let me know when you want it."

"I will telephone you from home when I've checked my diary." Charlie wrote out a cheque while John looked around the sales area. The vicar was always anxious to add a new acquisition to his antique oak collection.

"Anything new in? Any old oak I might like?"

"No John, sorry. I'm just restoring some old gilt picture frames and I've recently bought a Fityzroy barometer, a small pewter timepiece and a German Polyphon, but all three need some work on them."

After the customers left his shop, Chris stopped the lacquer clock, let down the gut lines and took of the weights and pendulum. When he moved the clock for delivery, it was essential the gut lines were fully unwound or they would spring and get tangled in the wheels of the clock movement.

When the shop was empty again, the dealer checked he had a suitable Mercury tube in stock to restore the Fitzroy barometer. It had been a busy day and he needed to relax so he called at the Barrowick Arms for a drink. Sara was serving at the bar.

She greeted him cheerily. "Hello. Nice to see you again."

"You too. I just fancy a pint of your best bitter. It's been a bit of a day."

Sara pulled a pint, handed it to him and leaned on the bar. "Why? Where have you been?"

"I've been back to Steve's place buying antiques."

"Are Dawn and Steve OK?"

"Sort of. They have business worries at the moment. I wish I could help them but it's difficult."

The barmaid nodded she understood and changed the subject. "Did you buy anything?"

"Yes, a few items."

"Any jewelry that I might be interested in?"

He knew since he'd bought her a Georg Jensen brooch at auction, she had become very interested in good class jewelry. "No. No jewelry, just a clock, a damaged barometer a mirror and a Polyphon."

The girl grimaced at this list. She wasn't into clocks or barometers. "I know you love your clocks but as far as I'm concerned a simple wristwatch will do for me."

He laughed at her comment and sipped his beer. As he sat quietly enjoying his drink, four fishermen came into the pub and ordered food from the bar. Sara was kept busy then and had little time to talk to him.

Chris finished his pint and walked home. It had been a busy day and he needed to relax and unwind. He sat in his favourite chair and read the Antique Trade Gazette to catch up on the latest auction results.

## Chapter Nineteen.

After his trip to Cromer and the handing over of the fake diamonds, Chris heard nothing from Steve for three days. Early one morning he received a phone call.

"Chris. Trouble I'm afraid. The Cromer gang are not happy with the stones you returned to them. They are insisting they were expecting some valuable diamonds and want to know what I've done with them."

Chris stood in silence and mulled this information over.

Steve spoke again. "Chris...are you there? Did you hear what I said?"

"Yes, I heard you. I gave them the diamonds as I found them. It's not my fault they expected more."

"They've had the stones valued and have been told they are just glass crystal of no real value."

Chris chose his words carefully. "It's not my fault if their associate duped them into believing he had valuable diamonds. They'll have to look elsewhere for their culprit. What about the widow? Any chance she has still got the real thing?"

Steve hesitated. "I don't know, Chris. I am only telling you what Barry Montgomery told me this morning. He hinted at all sorts of retribution if I don't return the diamonds to him."

Chris cursed silently to himself. He might have anticipated this but he had banked on the gang not knowing about the real stones. He could do nothing but bluff it out. "I gave them the things I found in that writing slope. If their mate misleads them, it is hardly my fault or yours, for that matter. Are you OK with it?"

"I'm not sure. They did hint they would take it out on Dawn, so I am worried about it."

Chris thumped his fist on the table. His mate was too far away in Norfolk for him to get over there quickly to help him out in an emergency. This was all going very wrong.

Steve came back on the phone. "Must go. Dawn has just returned from the shops. I don't want her hearing all this and worrying unnecessarily. I'll be in touch." With that promise Steve rang off, leaving Chris holding his phone and struggling to come up with any useful ideas.

After the disturbing news from Steve, Chris decided to start restoring the Admiral Fitzroy barometer. It would take his mind off the problem. He knew he always thought more clearly when he had something to do with his hands; just sitting and fretting wasn't his style.

He stripped out the broken mercury tube and removed the traces of old Mercury, before dusting it over the dustbin with a stiff brush. The printed scales were covered in an accumulation of dust that spoke of years of neglect. A soft paint brush removed most of that layer of dirt. Finally, he refreshed the mahogany carving on the case by brushing melted beeswax into the wood and polishing it off with a soft cloth. The weather tube, which was mercifully intact with all its contents sealed inside, just needed a wash in cold soapy water then fixing onto the wooden case. He checked his stock of old barometer tubes to find one that fitted the case and looked to be the right sort of date.

Barometer tubes are filled with Mercury, which is a metal that is liquid at room temperature and can be volatile, giving off poisonous fumes if heated. That is why the EU banned the production of new mercury barometers, but it was still legal to restore antique ones. Chris knew that the classic example of Mercury poisoning was met in the past in the hat making trade. Mercury salts were used to treat the felt that was made into hats. They treated the felt by heating it, but this gave off Mercury vapour. Hat makers inhaled these fumes and were prone to the neurological damage caused by it. The condition was referred to as Mad Hatters' Disease. It was a common industrial disease in Victorian times and was the inspiration for the character of the Mad Hatter in the Alice in Wonderland story.

Chris was well aware of the dangers of working with Mercury and always handled it in the open air. In any case, he reasoned, Mercury metal was not as volatile as heated mercury salts. He filled the glass tube with the correct amount of Mercury then inverted it to form a vacuum in the sealed end. The tube was then fixed in the wooden case, against the printed scale, to show the correct barometric pressure reading.

A telephone call to the local weather station at Cottesmore, a village a few miles from Barrowick with a large military base and a weather station, got him an up to date and accurate reading of the barometric pressure. He adjusted the mercury level and the scale accordingly.

This work took him most of the morning allowing him time to mull over the problem that Steve had outlined to him. He came to the conclusion that there was nothing more he could do; his reaction would depend on what the Cromer gang decided to do next. He was hoping they would stop chasing the diamonds, believing they already had what had been hidden in the antique writing slope He hoped they would stop bothering Steve and Dawn. Best left to stew, he thought; best to let them come to terms with their loss.

Just before lunchtime, when he was still working on the Fitzroy barometer, the shop bell rang, announcing a customer. He washed his hands and went into the sales area to see if he could help.

"Oh! Hello Tania. This is a surprise. What brings you over from Uppingham?"

Tania Wilkes stood in the showroom looking around at the stock he had for sale.

Chris couldn't help noticing how unusually smart she looked, in a summer dress and high heel shoes instead of the jeans and trainers she always wore when she was working. He'd never seen her looking so attractive. "Going somewhere special? You do look smart." He complimented the girl and smiled appreciatively at her.

"No, nowhere special, just come over to see you and visit your shop. I haven't been here before and thought it was about time I visited you at your workplace; after all, you have seen me at work many times"

He understood what she said but he was a little puzzled by this explanation. It did seem unusual for her to come over from Uppingham just to visit his shop. He smiled again. "Well, now you are here what do you think? Barrowick is not a busy place, not as busy as Uppingham. But it suits me and I am building up a regular clientele."

Tania smiled back at him. "You seem to have settled in well. It must seem very different to your old shop in Stamford."

Slightly embarrassed by her attention, Chris showed her around the showroom showing her the stock he had for sale. "No jewelry, I'm afraid. I do tend to deal mainly in furniture, especially clocks and barometers."

"You mentioned jewelry...that reminds me... what about that brooch you took the diamonds from and wanted glass crystals to repair it? Have you managed to do it? I thought I might help as I'm here."

Chris was taken aback at these comments. He was taken completely by surprise and had to think quickly what brooch she was referring to. "Ah! The glass crystals you kindly gave me, yes...yes...I glued them into the brooch and sold it into the trade." He hoped this explanation would satisfy her but he knew he had hesitated a bit too long with his answer and she would probably doubt this explanation.

"OK. Glad you managed to salvage the brooch. Did you manage to sell those two diamonds?"

"No, not yet." He lied. He felt that the less people knew about the diamonds the better. "I have sent them to Birmingham to a jewelry auction but they haven't been catalogued yet."

158

Tania just smiled. It may have been his guilty conscience at telling her those white lies, but he was sure she didn't believe him. It didn't really matter what Tania thought, he reminded himself, but he still felt a little guilty having to make up stories to keep the true extent of the diamonds a secret.

Tania browsed around the shop, stopping frequently to ask a question about the stock and to smile at him. He was beginning to feel slightly embarrassed at the attention she was giving him. Finally, he looked at his watch and said. "Time I was thinking about some lunch. I close the shop for my lunch hour and usually go out to eat."

"Oh good. Where do you have your lunch? You go to the Barrowick Arms I suppose, as it's your local."

"Well yes, usually. It suits me as it's so nearby and I don't have to go into town or cook something for myself."

"Good, I was thinking of trying the place myself. We can go together."

Chris shrugged his shoulders. "Why not." But he was beginning to feel the attention Tania was paying him was not entirely innocent. It did seem unusual for her to call on him and to be dressed so attractively. Now she was inviting herself to join him for lunch. "I will just have to go up to the flat and clean up a bit. Won't be many minutes."

Upstairs in his flat, he changed from his work clothes and washed his hands while Tania carried on looking around the sales area. Chris couldn't help but feel the girl had made a great effort to impress him, even using make up and dressing nicely. He admitted she was attractive and the sort of girl he would have dated, had he not been pleased with Sara's company.

He had no intention of getting involved seriously with anyone at that stage in his life and the open arrangement he had with Sara seemed to suit them both.

At the pub, he showed Tania to a table for two in a corner of the bar and gave her the menu. When she had decided what she fancied for lunch, he went to the counter to order their meals. Sara was not at the bar and her mother took the order.

"Sara not in?"

"She's out the back. She'll be here in a minute or two."

Chris returned to Tania and chatted to her about his business, about up and coming sales and enquired how her jewelry business was doing. Eventually Sara came over to their table bearing their order.

"Ah! Thanks Sara. I wondered where you were?" Chris smiled at his friend

Tania reached over patted Chris' hand and spoke to Sara. "We both wondered where you had got to."

Sara glanced down at their hands and frowned. He noticed her expression and quickly pulled his hand away. He turned in his chair to face the barmaid. "Tania called at the shop on business and as it was lunch time, she decided to try your catering."

Sara said nothing. She just walked away without a comment or a parting smile. Tania smiled to herself, a secretive little smile. Chris sighed and frowned even deeper. He did not like the games some women played, especially when he was involved without even realising it.

The meal passed silently between Chris and Tania. He knew what Tania was up to and only hoped Sara understood the situation. Tania was a crafty young lady. Her comment the previous week about needing a boyfriend like him, kept coming back to his mind.

After the meal was over, Tania said goodbye, returned to her car and drove back to Uppingham. Chris ordered another pint at the bar and tried to chat to Sara but she was not in a friendly mood. She ignored him, kept very busy serving other customers and drying the newly washed glasses. It was obvious, even to him, that Sara was upset by Tania's presence and her behaviour. He walked back to his shop deep in thought. He had believed his arrangement with Sara was platonic and suited them both, but now he wasn't so sure. These altered circumstances gave him some food for thought.

"Women can be so unpredictable!" He muttered to himself as he unlocked the shop door and let himself in, but he had little time to dwell on that thought. He noticed there was a recorded message on his telephone. When he listened to that recording, all thoughts of Sara and Tania Wilkes were driven from his mind. He was shocked to hear Steve's message.

"Hello Chris, it's Steve. Sorry to bother you again but things here are getting worse here. Last night someone slashed all four tyres on our car so I can't get out to do any business until I get the tyres replaced. Give me a ring if you have any suggestions about what I can do."

He rang Steve back as soon as he heard the message. "Steve. It's Chris. You say someone vandalised your car last night. Any ideas who?"

"Oh! I know who. It's got to be Montgomery and his mates. There's no way they are letting this diamond business drop. Any ideas mate?"

161

Chris agreed. It sounded more than likely it was the Cromer gang, but he had no useful suggestions to make.

Steve continued with his problems. "There's something else. Montgomery came to the shop yesterday afternoon when Dawn was out shopping, and threatened us both. He said if I didn't produce the missing stones, Dawn will get it; whatever that means. I'm worried Chris. I was beside myself with worry until Dawn returned from shopping. I can take care of myself but I can't be with Dawn all the time; she has her own life to lead. I'm very worried. I don't know what to do."

Chris cursed to himself. Why had he ever got his old friend involved in the diamond business? He tried to sound reassuring. "We haven't got any diamonds, have we. They will have to realise that fact, which I'm sure they will, sooner or later."

"The sooner the better as far as I'm concerned." Steve sounded very down.

"Do you want me to come over and speak with this chap? I can only tell him you haven't any diamonds. He'll have to believe us eventually."

"No, I don't think that will help Chris. I really don't know what to do. I can look after myself but I fear for my wife...I shall have to go now. I can hear Dawn coming into the office." He put the phone down abruptly and ended the call.

Chris stood for some minutes considering the situation. Surely Barry Montgomey and his associates wouldn't dare attack an innocent housewife like Dawn. He tried to convince himself it would all settle down given time but he knew the gang had tried searching his shop at Barrowick had broken into the Reverend Smyth's house to steal his writing slope. They were desperate. The fact they hadn't brought the police into the situation, considering Montgomery had contacts in the Norfolk force, only reinforced Chris' fears they were into something criminal and that may lead them to do something dangerous. He felt they were likely to take the law into their own hands, but he wouldn't voice that fear to Steve. He racked his brains but there seemed no solution to the problem. He silently cursed himself for ever getting involved with the Norfolk gang but he knew he couldn't turn back the clock. 'You can't saw sawdust' was a saying his apprentice master often used when he was a lad training to be a cabinet-maker. It was very true.

The phone rang again and Steve was back on the line. "Sorry about that. Dawn has gone out again so we can talk freely. Have you come up with any ideas?"

"No more ideas, Steve. I've given them back the stones I found in the writing slope. There's nothing more to be done." Chris felt very guilty telling his mate that lie but he knew he was in too deep to backtrack on his story.

"OK mate. Just needed to confide in someone I can trust. I daren't tell Dawn what he said; she would be devastated." Steve rang off again, leaving Chris with a lot to mull over.

The rest of that afternoon he spent finishing small restoration jobs. He carried on restoring the swept picture frames, which he'd had from the local auction house. He prepared the pieces of missing plaster moulding by making plasticine moulds of sound pieces and filling them with fine Plaster of Paris. He cut lengths of the moulding to fill the gaps on the frames then painted them with Burnt Umber paint as a base coat. Once the pieces were glued into place and the undercoat was dry, he painted the new pieces with gold leaf paint adding dark oil paint here and there to match the colour of the existing mouldings on the frames. It was precise work. The attention to detail demanded his undivided attention, which was just what he needed to take his mind off Steve's problems. When the frames were completed and left to dry, he searched the workshop for some other projects to fill in his time.

With the picture frames drying, Chris started on the Art Nouveau mirror he had picked up at Betty Crawford's antique warehouse in Norfolk. It was a mahogany wall mirror with an applied Art Nouveau design made in beaten Copper. He removed the mirror and the metal design of curved leaves and irises, then cleaned the wooden frame.

The mahogany frame of the mirror was sound but the surface French polish was badly scratched and needed stripping. Methylated spirit and fine wire wool made short work of the old finish. Once it had dried, he French polished it again to bring out the rich pattern of the wood grain.

The metal, which was formed into a floral Art Nouveau design, just needed careful cleaning then polishing with metal polish on a mop head. Satisfied with the finish, he sprayed it with clear lacquer and re-fixed it to the wooden frame with fine copper tacks.

One hour later the mirror was thoroughly cleaned and back in its frame. The polish just needed to harden before he contacted Mrs Gibbs to tell her he had found another piece of Art Nouveau for her decor.

By teatime, Chris was at a loose end. He had so much on his mind he decided to close the shop early and go to the Barrowick Arms for a drink.

At the pub, Sara was behind the bar tidying the shelves. She glanced up when he went into the bar but didn't bother to greet him as she usually did. The girl went into the kitchen and sent her mother out to serve him.

"Pint of bitter please, Mrs Goodacre."

The landlady pulled him a pint and placed it on the bar in front of him.

"Is Sara OK?" He enquired.

"You tell me. She seems very upset with you."

"Oh! I see." Chris didn't know what else to say. Obviously, the business with Tania Wilkes had upset the girl. He began to understand that Sara was taking their relationship a lot more seriously than he had realised. He took his beer to an empty table by the window and sat down. "Women!" He whispered the word quietly to himself. "Why must they take things so personal?'" He sipped his beer and gazed out of the window. Suddenly he was brought out of his reverie by the sound Sara's voice. She stood at his side holding out her hand.

Chris smiled at her. "Sara. Nice to see you."

She ignored his greeting and held out her hand towards him. "Here. You'd better have this back. Maybe Tania Wilkes would like it." She threw the Georg Jensen brooch onto the table and stalked back to the bar.

"Sara!" Chris called after her, but she ignored his call and vanished into the kitchen.

"Damn me!" He drained his glass and picked up the

small silver wren.  If that was the way she want ed it, he would let her get on with it.  He would never understand women.  His past experience with his ex wife had been a taste of how devious they could be, but he was not prepared for Sara behaving so childishly.  He had told her the arrangement with Tania was just business but she chose to disbelieve him.  As far as he was concerned, enough was enough.  He pocketed the silver brooch, left the pub and walked back to his shop.

Maybe it was because he was uptight about Steve and Dawn or maybe it was the bad memories of the hassle he had with Vickie, his ex wife, but Chris was determined he would not bother with Sara again.  He took the Georg Jensen brooch from his pocket and put it in a prominent place in the front of the shop window.  At least he could sell it and get his outlay back. If Sara didn't appreciate his gift, someone else was sure to like it and would buy it.

## Chapter Twenty

The day after the unfortunate incident with Sara, Chris was still of the same mind. He was mad that she should doubt him as she had and was determined to forget her. He checked the picture frames and the mirror he had restored the previous day and was pleased to find the work was fine. He put one of the frames, which would hold a standard sized canvas and would appeal to local artists, on display in his shop window and wrapped the remainder in bubble wrap to keep them from getting damaged. When he had stored the frames in his workshop, he turned his attention to the Art Nouveau mirror. The work he had done on the mahogany frame and the copper design was satisfactory, and the French-polish had hardened. He cleaned the glass of the mirror again and decided he would contact Veronica Gibbs and take it over to show her.

When he arrived in Uppingham at the Gibbs' house, Veronica answered the door dressed only in her dressing gown.

167

"I've just had a shower." She assured him. "Do come in and show me the mirror."

He followed the woman into the house and into the spare room, carrying the mirror for her.

"Put it over there. There is a picture hook that should hold it." She pointed to a bare wall beside the guest bed.

He dutifully placed the mirror on the wall and stepped back to let his client see the effect.

"Wonderful Christopher. I knew you wouldn't fail me." She stood in front of the mirror and opened her dressing gown, letting it drop to the floor around her ankles.

The dealer took a step back and turned away from her, trying to look anywhere but at her naked figure. He wasn't embarrassed, but he didn't want to encourage her in any way. She took her opportunity and pushed him back onto the bed, falling on top of him as he landed. "Oh! I am sorry Christopher. What must I be thinking?" But she made no effort to move off him.

He gently extricated himself from Veronica's embrace and walked to the door. "I'll leave the bill in the hall, Mrs Gibbs. I'm glad you like the mirror."

Veronica lay on the bed and just pouted at him. "You are no fun Christopher. I am disappointed. Anyway I think the mirror will look better in the main bedroom. Take it down and follow me upstairs."

Reluctantly, he retrieved the mirror and followed Veronica up to her bedroom. She hadn't bothered to put her dressing gown back on and preceded him completely naked, up the stairs and into the front bedroom.

"Try it over there." She pointed to a space on the wall

168

overlooking the king-sized bed.

He obliged by holding the mirror in place.

Mrs Gibbs sat on the bed and directed him to move the mirror along the wall until she seemed satisfied with the position of it. "Now Christopher, if you mark the spot I will get a hammer and a picture hook and you can fix it in position for me." She ran down the stairs and returned immediately with the tools for the job.

Chris hammered the picture hook into the wall and hung the mirror. "That OK?" he asked her.

"Come over here beside me on the bed and let me look properly."

Reluctantly he joined her and sat on the edge of the duvet.

"Sit back here and let me see." She pulled him back, climbed onto him and pretended to look at their reflection in the mirror. She obviously wanted the mirror placed to reflect the scene on her bed.

"Well? Is it OK?" Chris was getting fed up with her advances and let her know it by the tone in his voice.

She sighed deeply. "Yes, just right. I was only thinking, if we were to have it off now we could both catch the action in that new mirror."

Chris gently extricated himself from her embrace.

"Oh! You are strong, Christopher. I like strong men." She made no attempt to get up from the bed or to cover herself.

He shook his head and frowned. It was good paying business selling to the Gibbs, but he was beginning to regret dealing with them. "I must go. I've another delivery to make

169

locally." He lied to get away from her.

Veronica Gibbs just shook her head in frustration but made no attempt to move.

Chris left the house and went back to his van, glad to have escaped from that woman. It wasn't that he was immune to female charms but mixing business with pleasure and getting involved with a client was not a good idea. In any event, Veronica wasn't his type or his age group. Thoughts of female company and the realisation he had probably fallen out irrevocably with Sara Goodacre, reminded him of how that had happened. He smiled to himself. Maybe he should call on Tania Wilkes while he was In Uppingham. The least he would get was a coffee and she would be pleased to see him, of that he was sure.

When the dealer arrived at Tania's home, he found her busy polishing her latest jewelry commissions. She stopped the buffing wheel immediately, took off her protective gloves and eye shield and greeted him "Lovely to see you again, Chris. On your own this time Sara not with you?"

He couldn't resist a wry smile. Tania had done her best to upset his arrangement with Sara. She was fully aware of the effect she had had at the Barrowick Arms when they took lunch there together. Sometimes women could be so devious. He shouldn't have been surprised after his married years with Vickie. He smiled and answered her questions.

"Yes, on my own. Sara has decided to cool our relationship a bit. Not that it was that serious anyway."

"Good...I mean good to see you again. What brings you over to Uppingham this time? More diamonds to value? Another broken brooch to repair?"

170

"No. I was delivering a mirror to a customer this way and decided to call on you for a free coffee."

"I see. Well it's about time I had a break." She went over to the sink, washed her hands then switched on her percolator. "Where have you been delivering this time?"

"Veronica Gibbs place. She has just bought an Art Nouveau mirror from me."

"Ah! The delectable Veronica! Did you get away unscathed? She has a certain reputation with all the young tradesmen locally. My plumber is petrified of her and he's well over six feet tall! He even took his young daughter with him the last time he did a job at her house. " She laughed aloud.

"She's not my type or my age group. She did try, but she's always trying. They are good payers and business is business so I put up with the hints. I just feel a bit sorry for her old man."

"Don't feel sorry for him! He has a bit on the side, if local gossip is to be believed."

The dealer grinned. Village life was often like that and everybody knew the best- kept secrets.

"Anyway, you don't need an excuse to call on me. You know you are welcome any time." Tania smiled and handed him his coffee. "Would you like a biscuit?" She held out a tin of mixed biscuits for him to choose. They drank in sociable silence, enjoying the break from business and relaxed in each other's company. At last Tania spoke again.

"So, you and Sara are no longer an item then?" It was a tentative question and left more unsaid.

He nodded. The implications of her question were not

171

lost on him.

"I have two tickets for a concert at the Uppingham theatre tomorrow night. Would you care to come?"

He was pleasantly surprised at this invitation. It would make a change from his nightly visits to the Barrowick Arms, which were now proving embarrassing with Sara's attitude towards him. "Yes...that's kind of you, Tania. I'd love to come. You must let me pay you for the ticket."

"No problem. I was given them anyway by one of my rich business contacts."

"Lucky you. Sure, he won't mind you taking another bloke along?"

Tania laughed out loud and nearly spilled her coffee. "He's a she! And she's happily married anyway."

Chris joined in her laughter. He realised he had made several wrong assumptions about his companion. She was attractive and he'd assumed it was a male who had given her the tickets.

After they had finished their coffee and biscuits Chris got up to leave.

"Hang on a minute. There was something you could do for me." Sara stopped him leaving.

"Anything I can do, I will. You've been a great help to me on numerous occasions." He sat down again.

"I am looking for some old tools. There's a particular type of pliars used for forming circles in silver or gold wire." She went over to her toolbox and took out an example. "Like this pair but much smaller. I need them for filigree wirework and no one seems to make them any more. If you see a pair in your travels, at some country auction, get them for me. I'll pay

172

a good price for them because I really need them."

"I do know of a dealer in rare tools. He's over at Fulbeck Hall in Lincolnshire. If I get over that way, I'm sure he'll have some. I'll look out for you."

She showed him the pliers again and stressed the size she was looking to find. He nodded he understood her needs then left the studio to drive back to Barrowick. On his way home, he called at the new petrol station and the M&S convenience store on the Oakham bypass to fill up his petrol tank and to buy some sandwiches and a drink for his evening meal as he no longer felt welcome at his local pub.

That evening he sat in his flat, seated in his favourite chair by the French windows, looking out over Rutland Water. The sandwiches and soft drink he had bought at the convenience store had satisfied his hunger but they weren't up to the standard of his usual meal at the Barrowick Arms. Women can be funny creatures; he ruminated on the way Sara had behaved and the way Tania had quickly stepped into her shoes. After his unfortunate marriage and divorce, he was wary of commitment but, he had to admit, he did like female company. Bless them, he thought, faults and all. Where would we be without them?

## Chapter Twenty-One

The following evening,  the dealer had a leisurely shower after his day's work, put on his smartest casual clothes and drove over to Tania Wilkes's home.  He arrived an hour before they were due at the theatre and found Tania was still in the shower.

"Help yourself to a drink." She shouted. "I won't be a minute."

Chris poured himself a glass of red wine from the bottle Tania had thoughtfully put on a side table, and sat in her lounge admiring the artwork she had on her walls. Eventually she came out of the bathroom, dressed in a towelling dressing gown and joined him.

"Sorry I'm not quite ready, but we have plenty of time. The theatre is only a ten-minute walk up the road from here." She sat next to him and sipped her wine.

174

He could smell her perfume and feel the warmth radiating from her body after her shower. It was exhilarating being in her company in such an intimate way. "I like the artwork. Local artists are they?" He waved his hand at the pictures surrounding them.

"Very local. They're all my work." She smiled at his compliment.

"I didn't know you painted. Have you trained in art?"

"Not exactly. I was going to do an art degree but changed my mind. "

"I think you could have made it as an artist, judging by these examples."

Tania smiled again. She valued his judgement. "I decided there were too many painters about and I would probably have finished up as an art teacher. I just didn't fancy teaching reluctant kids. As a jewelry designer I am one of a few such people locally and I don't have much competition. I think I made the right choice."

"So do I. You obviously have a good business sense as well as being a gifted artist."

When she had finished her drink, Tania left him admiring her paintings while she went to her bedroom to change. She eventually came back into the lounge looking radiant in a red evening dress.

"Sorry I didn't come in a dress suit." He apologised. "I didn't realise it would be formal dress code!"

"It's not." Tania assured him. "I just fancied making the evening special. Anyway, we women can get away with a formal attire, or just jeans, if we like. No one will bat an eyelid at my dress, you see."

Tania was right. Several of the ladies had taken the trouble to dress formally for the occasion and many of the younger women turned up in their jeans and sweaters. It was a very relaxed evening.

Just before the curtain went up for the start of the entertainment, Veronica Gibbs and her husband came into the theatre. Chris heard her raucous laughter from the front stalls and recognised it immediately. He turned to Tania and whispered, "Sounds like Veronica. Should have guessed she would be here."

The entertainment was billed as a one-man show. The entertainer, Bill Middleton, was a singer songwriter who specialised in humorous North Country songs, much as Jake Thackery used to perform. He accompanied his songs on acoustic guitar but he had a brought a double base player with him to swell the sound. The audience soon warmed to his humour, clapping and shouting after every number to show their appreciation. He enjoyed it immensely; it was a complete change for him to go to the theatre.

After the show, as they walked back to Tania's home, she linked her arm in his and snuggled up to him.

"Enjoy it, Chris?"

"I'll say. I like the northern sense of humour, and he can certainly play that guitar. Haven't had such an enjoyable evening in ages."

After a night drink and a goodnight kiss, Chris thanked Tania again for such a lovely evening then drove along the quiet dark roads back to his flat at Barrowick. The village was asleep when he drove up Main Street the only glimmers of light coming from chinks in the curtains where the sleepers

176

preferred to leave a light on all night. Even the Barrowick Arms was all in darkness.

As he slowly drove past the church a Fox crossed the road in front of his car. In the headlights he could see it was a mature dog fox. He slowed down to let the animal cross safely and watched it trot along the pavement on its nightly search for food. No doubt some of the locals put scraps out for it. In his flat, he made himself another night drink and went to bed. When one door closes another one opens, he thought. I guess that old saying is often proved correct.

## Chapter Twenty-Two

The morning after his night out at the Uppingham Theatre, Chris rose late. He had nothing planned for the day and intended to tidy his workshop and sort through the jobs awaiting his attention. Her needed to get them into some kind of order of priority. He still had an afterglow from the night before and from his outing with Tania. She was a talented and attractive girl, and a pleasure to be with. The postman called that morning bringing him a tracked letter, which had to be signed for. It contained the cheque from the Birmingham jewelry auction. The dealer couldn't resist a wry smile when he read the amount of the cheque. Fifty thousand pounds was some windfall. He was on a high when the phone rang, but everything changed in that instant!

" Hello Steve. What can I do for you this morning?"

"I need help, Chris. I think Montgomery and his mates may have kidnapped Dawn!"

178

Chris was immediately concerned. He put the cheque down on the table and gave his full attention to his friend's call. "Tell me exactly what's happened, Steve."

"She's not been home last night. Yesterday she went into town to do some shopping and she hasn't returned. I've sat up all night worried sick about her. I've rung the hospital and the police but drawn a blank with both."

"Maybe she's at a mates?" Chris desperately tried to be positive.

"No. She would have rung me."

"Of course. Sorry. Just trying to be helpful. Do you want me to come over to Cley? Two heads are better than one. We might get more done together."

Steve was silent on the phone.

Chris asked him again. "You still there, Steve? I'll come straight over. OK?"

"I'm worried sick about her. They threatened her before, you know. I wish I'd never heard of those bloody diamonds!"

The dealer ended the call and closed his shop before he set out in his van for his local bank to deposit the £50,000 cheque then he drove straight to the Norfolk coast. By the time he arrived in Cley his friend had made further enquiries about his wife and had managed to find one of Dawn's friends who had seen her on the quayside at Wells. She wasn't alone when the friend saw her. From the description of the man who was with her, Steve realised it must have been Barry Montgomery. His worst fears were realised.

Chris parked his van next to Steve's antique shop and hurried inside. He found his friend on the telephone.

Steve slammed down the phone and turned to face his

friend. "I was right. I've just had a threatening phone call telling me they have Dawn and they will not return her until they get their diamonds back."

"Ring the police." Chris suggested.

"Can't. They just warned me she will never some back alive if I do bring the police into it. Anyway, Barry Montgomery has his contacts in the local police so he's bound to hear of it if I do ring them. "

Steve collapsed into a chair, his head in his hands. "What am I going to do? I don't have their diamonds and they have Dawn. If they harm her I'll murder them!"

Chris stood by his friend and considered the situation. It was very serious. The drug gang had already taken to violence and wouldn't hesitate to do it again. He tried to offer some cool advice to his friend.

"We must talk to that girl who saw Dawn with a man. Get to know exactly what she saw, when and where she witnessed it. Maybe she can help us track Dawn down."

Steve raised his head and nodded. He had tears in his eyes but a determined look on his face. "She said she saw Dawn at Wells but my wife had no reason to go there today. I'll ring Josie back and get all the information I can."

By the time Steve came off the phone from Josie he had a much better picture of what she had seen. "Josie saw Dawn at the quayside in Wells. She saw her get onto a fishing boat and go into the cabin. From the description of the man accompanying her, it was definitely Barry Montgomery. I think we'd better drive to Wells and see what's going on."

Chris wasted no more time. He drove his friend to Wells Next the Sea and parked near the sea front. When they arrived there they found there were no boats moored in the harbour; the whole fishing fleet was out crab fishing, as the conditions were ideal for it. Steve searched the local pubs looking for someone he might know. Finally, he found a local lad who had occasionally sold him some small antiques.

"We are looking for Barry Montgomery. He keeps a boat here we understand."

"So, he does. He might be at the quay, but if his boats gone he's probably off fishing down the coast. It's a good day for it."

Steve turned to his mate and shook his head. "Looks as if we've missed him. Wherever he is, he has my wife with him. The bastard had better not harm her or I'll kill him!"

Chris led Steve out of the pub and drove him back to his shop in Cley.

"Dammit! I'm going to ring the police and tell them Dawn is missing." Steve paced up and down the kitchen, unable to settle.

Chris said nothing. Dawn had not been missing for long and they had no proof she had been forced to accompany Barry Montgomery. The anonymous caller had warned against going to the police. Was that just an empty threat or would the kidnappers carry out their threats? He kept his thoughts to himself and didn't disclose his doubt to his friend as he knew they would fall on deaf ears.

Steve rang the local police who made a note of his call and told him to wait and see if his wife returned. "She may have just stayed with a friend." The constable suggested. When Steve mentioned the anonymous phone call the policeman didn't take it seriously. "Why would anyone want to harm your wife, Sir? We often get calls like this when there's been a domestic. Did you and your wife part company on friendly terms?"

Steve was livid. "Of course, we did! What do you take me for, a wife beater?"

The officer apologised but didn't seem to take the complaint very seriously. "Leave it to the morning, Sir. Let's see if she turns up tomorrow."

Steve couldn't bring himself to explain about the diamonds. It would sound too farfetched and unlikely. He got the impression, rightly so, that the local police thought he was a bit of a nuisance caller himself. They gave him a crime number and insisted he should wait to see if his wife returned in the next day or so.

Steve slammed down the phone and swore out loud. "I reckon they think my wife has left me for another bloke!"

Later that day they received another anonymous phone call repeating the threats to Dawn if the diamonds were not returned.

"I can't stand by and do nothing. I'll never forgive myself if anything happens to Dawn." Steve was beside himself with worry.

"Right. Let's consider what we can do. Any way of finding this boat of Barry Montgomery's? Is there anywhere else along the coast he could keep it?"

Steve shook his head. "I don't know. I'm not familiar with the local fishing fraternity,"

"Do you have any friends who would know?" Chris was desperately trying to sound positive and get his friend to do something other than panic.

182

"Yes. I have a mate at Kelling who sometimes helps with the crab fishing. I'll ring Ted."

When he came off the phone, Steve was even more frustrated. "Ted says as far as he knows Barry Montgomery only moors at Wells, but he has promised to sound out his fishing mates and get back to me."

Chris sat down and tried to take his friend's mind off their problems by discussing the antique trade with him. Suddenly the phone rang again. Steve jumped up to answer it.

"That's good of you to check for me. Thanks Ted."

Chris looked over expectantly at his friend.

"Ted says Montgomery's boat frequently goes along the coast and out into the North Sea out of sight of land. There are rumours he meets another boat out there and takes things on board from a larger vessel from the continent. He's going to try to get some location bearings for me. He'll contact his fishing mates."

"Good. Sounds promising. If someone wanted to hide Dawn it would be an ideal plan to ship her out to sea and anchor off the coast. His boat has gone somewhere secret and he might even be expecting a shipment of drugs from Holland or elsewhere on the continent."

"Drugs? What gives you that idea?"

"A few days ago, I was in Northampton and saw the skinny bloke who was arguing with you the day I bought the clock and the writing slope. He was meeting a known drug dealer and handing some items over to him. I'll bet my year's taking it was a drug transaction."

Steve nodded vigorously. "There have been rumours locally that someone was dealing in this area."

183

"It would explain why they need diamonds. They are a valuable and untraceable commodity, much smaller and lighter than precious metals, and acceptable anywhere, unlike some currencies." After some further thought Chris asked. "Do you know any boat owners? If we could locate Barry Montgomery's boat we might be able to persuade him to see sense and release Dawn."

Steve thumped his fist into his hand. "I'll persuade him! Just give me a chance." He fell silent then suddenly brightened up when he remembered a local contact from his days with the Paras. "Johnny Stevens runs a scuba diving school just up the coast from here. He must have a sea going boat as he dives on wrecks for treasure in the North Sea."

"Mad Johnny? Haven't seen him since my army days. "

Steve didn't wait to discuss the past, he rifled through a drawer in the desk looking for his address book. "Found it! I've got his phone number. He gave it to me recently at a regimental get together." Steve rang the number and waited for someone to answer.

"Hello." A woman answered the phone.

"Is Johnny there?"

"Who's calling?"

"Tell him it's Steve, Steve Edmund." Steve pressed the phone button to turn on the speaker so Chris could follow the conversation. After a few minutes a man's voice came over the phone.

"Steve. Nice to hear from you. What can I do for you?"

Chris shouted from his chair. "Johnny, it's Chris Doughty here."

" Good God! You got a Special Forces reunion going.

184

Why didn't you tell me, Steve?"

Steve ignored the banter and got straight to the point. "I'm in trouble Johnny. My wife's been kidnapped and we need a boat and some help."

The line went temporarily silent while Johnny absorbed this news. "Good grief, Steve, that sounds serious."

Chris got up from his chair. "Let me speak to him." He took the phone from his friend. "Johnny, we believe Dawn is being held on a fishing boat out in the North Sea. We know she was taken on board at Wells. We need someone with expertise in sea going boats and boarding vessels. Can you help?"

"I'll say! Just like old times in the specials. I'll be over to Wells within the hour. Just try to get a firm fix on the whereabouts of this boat and we can sort it." Johnny rang off leaving his two friends to try and learn the co-ordinates of Barry Montgomery's vessel.

Steve looked lost, so Chris took over. "Get me your fishing mate on the phone again. Let's see what we can find out from him."

Within the hour, he had found out that the missing boat was a large sea going vessel with decks fore and aft and a sizeable accommodation cabin. It was called the Molly and had that name emblazoned on the prow and across the front of the cabin. A few more phone calls and the co-ordinates of the last sighting of the vessel were given to him by one of the fishermen who had recently spotted the boat at anchor off the coast. Having learned all he could, Chris suggested he and Steve should go in his van to Wells to await Johnny Stevens' arrival.

As they stood on the quay at Wells waiting for Johnny to turn up on his boat, Chris asked, "What are we looking for? What sort of boat does Johnny own?"

Steve looked around the water at the few craft moored there. "It's a twin keeled boat with a rail around the front and a small cabin set close to the prow. I guess it's about thirty feet long and some six feet wide."

"What about colour or name?" Chris was looking out to sea, shielding his eyes from the glare of the sun.

"Mucky white colour from what I remember. I don't recall a name." Steve scratched his head trying to recall all he could about their friend's boat. "I do remember it had numerous round red buoys tethered to the sides of it. I suppose Johnny uses those when he's diving on sunken wrecks."

Chris agreed. "It must be sea going if he dives on offshore salvage sites. Is it a fast boat?"

"Ah! That I do know. He was bragging to me at the last meeting in Norwich. He has twin 150 horsepower motors. He reckons it could outrun almost anything on the water."

"Trust him! He always did live in the fast lane. That goes for his taste in girls as well. I don't suppose he's married yet, is he?"

"No, but he has had the same live in partner for several years now." Steve frowned as he concentrated on trying to recall the girl's name. "Naomi, yes that's her name, Naomi. Nice girl as well."

The pair remained on the quay looking out to sea while they waited for John Stevens and his boat to arrive.

Within the hour, as he had promised, John steered his

craft into Wells' harbour and moored her near his friends. Chris and Steve were pleasantly surprised to see how well equipped he was. The boat had diving equipment, inflatable dinghies and all the gear he used to teach scuba diving as well as searching for wrecks in the North Sea. The two powerful outboard motors were fixed on the back of it. Along the prow it displayed the name 'Naomi"

"Nice boat, Johnny." Chris shouted to his old mate.

"Should be, the amount I paid for her. It's a pity the bank still owns most of her."

Chris helped Steve step down onto the deck then the three men went forward into the cabin to talk.

"We've located the boat we think Dawn is being held on. It's the Molly and it's a sea going boat." Chris took a note from his pocket and gave Johnny the co-ordinates he had been given.

"That's some way out. Certainly, over the horizon and well out of sight of land."

"Is that a problem?" Steve sounded worried.

"No but any boat approaching it will be spotted long before it reaches it. That means waiting until after dark."

"What's the best way to tackle it, John?" Chris asked.

"That's where our army training comes in. I think we should anchor some way off the Molly and go in undercover of darkness, like we trained to do in the Specials." He turned to Chris ."You did the scuba training with me in the army, think you can still cut it?"

Chris hesitated. "I haven't done anything like that for over ten years. I'm not sure."

Johnny patted him on the back. "Trust me, It'll come

187

back when you put on the wet suit and get into the sea. It's like riding a bike, you never forget. Anyway, hopefully we should be able to use the inflatable to get right up to the boat and climb on board."

Chris wasn't so sure about his ability to swim in the North Sea but he just nodded agreement.

Steve was full of questions. "Will you be able to find the Molly in the dark?"

"If these co-ordinates are right my satellite navigation system will find her."

"What if they aren't correct?"

"Let's wait and see." Johnny tried to calm him down. "No good crossing bridges 'till we come to them. I have a good radar system on board so that should help."

"What will you do when you do find the Molly?"

"Let's wait and see. If we can get aboard without the crew noticing, it won't be a problem. Let's hope Dawn is OK and we can surprise them." He turned to Chris. "I have brought along a couple of side handle batons just in case things get violent."

## Chapter Twenty-Three.

As the evening progressed and the light began to fail, the Naomi left Wells harbour with the three friends on board. They headed out to sea towards the location where they hoped to find the Molly. It was fairly calm out at sea that night, which was a blessing, as bad weather would have made the task much more difficult. The twin-engine boat made fast progress and was soon in the area where Johnny hoped to find their quarry. He cut the lights as they approached, not wishing to be detected and frighten the crew of the other boat. He also cut one engine to reduce the noise level of their approach. The three men crowded into the small cabin to watch the radar screen.

Steve pointed to a dark shape picked up by the system. "That's the right shape. That could be the Molly."

"There's lights over there." Chris looked out of the cabin window and pointed ahead of them into the darkness

Johnny cut the engine and picked up his night scope binoculars. He searched the horizon. "That's her. I can see her name across the cabin top. That's our target. She's riding at anchor with all her lights on. She's lit up like a Christmas tree. I wonder why? Can't see any movement on deck at the moment."

He put down the glasses and turned to his two companions. "Time to get the wetsuits on, Chris. Then we can approach them slowly and quietly. We'll drop anchor on the Naomi, use the inflatable and hope we can board her unseen."

The two men slipped on the black wet suits, hung the batons at their sides and prepared the inflatable for launching. Suddenly Steve spoke in an urgent voice drawing their attention to an unexpected development.

"Look. There' a large boat pulling alongside the Molly."

Johnny looked at his companions. "What's going on? Did we expect this?"

"I think they are probably taking delivery of drugs. That's where we think they are making their money."

"Damn!" Johnny growled. "That means many more crew to deal with. Better think this out." After a brief silence he said. "We'll have to get closer before we board them. When we get close enough, Steve, I want you to fire off these two distress flairs." He handed the flairs to his friend.

"What are you thinking?" Chris asked.

"If we can fool them into thinking the coastguards are on to them, the large boat will scarper. The Molly will probably stay put and throw any drugs overboard. They'll know they can't outrun a coastguard boat."

"What about Dawn?" Steve could see problems. Maybe she would be put aboard the larger boat or they would get rid of her in some other way. "She is the victim of a kidnapping and could testify against them."

"You're right. We'd better not waste time." Johnny fired up both outboard motors and headed towards the two boats. "Fire those flairs Steve. Let's panic them."

Within minutes the fast boat was almost alongside the Molly. By the intense light from the flairs they could see the larger boat was already pulling away and making out to sea. Two men could be seen scurrying about the Molly's deck throwing bundles overboard.

"Take her up close, Chris. I'm going overboard to swim to her blind side." As soon as they were near enough, Johnny balanced on the side of the inflatable and dropped backwards into the water. Chris pulled alongside the Molly and cut the engines. He handed the controls over to Steve and jumped onto the deck of the Molly. Once on board he ran towards the cabin, where he hoped he would find Dawn safe and sound.

One of the crew, the thick set man who Chris immediately recognised as the man he'd met twice before, at Cley and at the sale room, jumped in front of him wielding a long-handled boathook. Chris dodged the first thrust and unhooked his baton from his belt. The man's second attempt was more successful. The sharp metal hook hit Chris across his left arm. The hook tore into his wet suit and drew blood. By the time the third blow was launched, he was ready for it. He dodged to one side and hooked the pole with his baton. Grabbing the pole, he pulled his attacker off balance.

The man dropped the boat hook and tried to grapple

191

with Chris but he hadn't reckoned on his adversary being armed with the baton. One swift blow to his neck, and Chris laid his assailant out cold on the deck. He was about to run to the cabin when a second man stepped out onto the deck holding a woman in front of him.

Chris hesitated, not sure what to expect.

"One more step and she gets it." Barry Montgomery had a gun in his hand and was pointing it at Dawn's head.

"Don't be daft man. Kidnapping is bad enough but murder will see you put away for life."

Dawn screamed and struggled but she was no match for the ex-policeman.

"One step nearer and you get it as well." Montgomery waved the pistol at Chris.

Chris stood his ground. The baton, which he still had in his right hand, he held behind his back out of sight. It was his only weapon,

"Get down on the deck." The gunman ordered

Chris hesitated. He had noticed a shadowy figure creeping up behind the gunman. He slowly sank to his knees.

"Get down!" Montgomery shouted again.

Suddenly the shadowy figure leapt into action. Johnny looped his baton over the gunman's head and pulled it across the man's throat. He pushed his knee into Montgomery's back and pulled the baton towards his chest.

Immediately, Chris leapt forward, swung his baton and smashed the pistol from the man's hand.

Montgomery let go of his captive and clutched at this throat but he couldn't dislodge Johnny's baton. He sank onto the deck, a gurgling sound coming from his constricted throat.

Dawn collapsed onto the deck as her assailant struggled to get free but he was no match for the ex para. Within minutes it was all over. Both crew members of the Molly were tied hand and foot and lay moaning on the deck.

Steve threw a rope to Johnny and tethered the Naomi alongside the Molly, then he jumped aboard. He rushed forward, enveloped his wife in his arms and comforted her.

Once the emergency was over, Chris became aware of the pain in his arm and the warm blood running down his hand. He felt the gaping wound and gripped his arm with a handkerchief to stem the flow of blood.

Johnny noticed what was happening. "We'd better get that dressed, Chris. Are you feeling OK? Not going to faint, are you? Hang on 'till we can get you back on the Naomi. I've got a first aid kit there."

The four of them were just getting back on the Naomi when the coastguard lifeboat pulled alongside. The flares they had sent into the night sky had alerted the RNLI and brought them quickly out to the scene.

"You alright mate?" A male voice hailed them from the lifeboat.

"We're OK now. But we have a couple of kidnappers and drug smugglers for you. They're on the deck of that boat, trussed up tight."

Once the lifeboat crew had boarded the Molly and been told what had happened that night they took Barry Montgomery and his mate on board. Johnny used his inflatable and recovered the parcels of drugs that were floating in the sea. He handed them over to the lifeboat crew. There was enough evidence gathered to put the whole gang

193

behind bars for a long time. Drug smuggling and kidnapping crimes were just the beginning of their problems.

Back on shore Dawn soon recovered. Chris had the wound on his arm dressed but it was deeper than he anticipated and he couldn't stop the bleeding; he had to be taken to the local hospital to have it stitched. Afterwards, the three friends sat in Steve's kitchen drinking coffee into the small hours of the morning and winding down from the night's excitement.

"Just like old times." Johnny declared. " Do you miss the old days in the Paras?"

"Not me." Steve shook his head emphatically.

"Or me." Chris sat nursing his sore arm. "I said goodbye to all that years ago."

Johnny reluctantly nodded agreement, but he didn't look convinced. "I suppose I agree with the pair of you, but it was good to meet up again and get the adrenaline flowing." He took his mobile phone from his pocket and rang his girlfriend to reassure her everything was alright, then he returned to his friends. "Chris, you'll have to come over to Norwich next time we have our get together. We can put you up at my place, we've got a spare bed. It's a double so you can bring along your lady friend, if you have one."

Chris grinned and cradled his damaged arm. "I'm not sure my health will stand too much of your company."

They all broke into laughter. Even Dawn had recovered enough to join in with them.

## Chapter Twenty-Four

The wound in Chris' arm did cause him some problems.
It limited his ability to drive long distances. For a week after
he had the wound stitched he stayed in the Barrowick area
and didn't venture far afield. He had plenty to keep him
occupied and caught up with all his restoration work. His
only problem was where to go to eat as he was avoiding his
local pub and meeting Sara. Finally, one evening, he put his
concerns to one side and ventured down to the Barrowick
Arms.

Mrs Goodacre was running the bar.

"A Beer and some sandwiches, please. " He smiled at the
landlady and looked around the bar to see is Sara was about.

"Ham suit you, Chris?" She pulled him a pint and
placed it in front of him.

"Sara not in?".

"No. She's out with her new boyfriend. You remember
Derek Brown, the lad who played the guitar at our last folk
night. She's out with him."

Chris smiled. He was pleased Sara was moving on.

The landlady continued. "Those two have a lot in common, with their music, and they are of a similar age."

Chris took the hint. He was several years older than Sara and had never considered their relationship to be very serious. "Good. I'm glad she's Ok." He took his beer and sandwiches to a table in the far corner of the bar to eat and drink in peace. Now he knew what was happening, he felt he could continue to use the pub as his local without too much ill feeling. He mused over the comments about age and realised Tania was much nearer his age. Things had a way of working themselves out.

Two weeks after the eventful night out a sea, when he'd had his stitches removed and his arm was recovering well, Chris went back to Cley to visit Steve and his wife. He had been in daily touch with them by phone since the escapade but he hadn't mentioned the diamonds or the money they had made at auction. He set out early in the morning, but he wasn't alone. This time he took Tania Wilkes with him.

"I thought a day by the sea might repay you for that excellent concert you took me to." He explained.

Tania jumped at the invitation and the chance of a leisurely day away from work, especially as it was an opportunity to be with Chris.

"We can call on an old mate of mine to do a bit of business then go on to Cromer for lunch. How's that suit you?"

She readily agreed.

He drove the van to Cley and parked in the yard next to Steve's antique business. His friend and Dawn were out of the door to greet them before either of them stepped down

Dawn showed her surprise when she came face to face with Tania. Steve, aware of his wife's expression, rushed in to defuse the situation. "Lovely to see you Chris and you er.." He searched for a name.

Chris filled the gap. "Tania...Tania Wilkes. She's a jewelry designer from Uppingham. I owed her a day out for the many business favours she's done for me."

Steve shook hands with the girl and winked at Chris. "Business favours eh? Do come in. We were waiting for you to arrive before we stopped work for our coffee break."

Chris ushered Tania into the small kitchen and sat down at the table. "How are you, Dawn? Fully recovered?"

Dawn just smiled and nodded. She didn't elaborate on his comments. Steve had impressed on her the less she discussed the kidnapping the better. Her loose talk about diamonds had already caused them untold problems and could have cost her her life.

Chris was pleased at this reticence. He hadn't discussed the events with Tania and didn't want to have to explain those things to her. He drank his coffee and turned to Steve.

"Show me those antiques you have in the barn, Steve." He winked at his old friend to get him to play along with his suggestion.

"Right, follow me."

Chris smiled at Tania. "Stay here and talk to Dawn. Old furniture can be a messy business."

The two men went to the outbuilding where Steve stored his latest purchases that needed some work on them. As soon as they were inside and the door closed behind them, he turned to Chris. " You know I haven't any money to buy

197

antiques, so I don't know what you hope to see out here. What was that all about?"

"It's about this." Chris handed him a cheque for £25,000.

Steve looked shocked. "What's this?'

"Your half share in the diamonds."

Steve read the amount on the cheque and whistled in amazement. "What diamonds? I thought you said they were worthless glass crystals."

"Yes. I did say that. I was hoping to fool your local gang, but it didn't work."

Steve frowned and took a step back. "And Dawn reaped the result!"

"Yes. I deeply regret that, but if she hadn't blabbed about the stones in the first place none of that would have happened."

Steve stayed silent for some seconds mulling over the situation then he nodded agreement. "Of course. You're right." He read the cheque amount once again and grinned. "This will get us out of a hole. I really thought we would have to sell up and go bust. Thanks mate." He folded the cheque and put it safely in his wallet.

"What are mates for?" Chris slapped Steve on his back.

"That's exactly what Johnny said when I bumped into him recently in Norwich. He sends his regards, by the way. I think he's getting very nostalgic about our army days. That taste of danger has reminded him of old times."

The two men returned to the girls and had more coffees. Nothing was said about the money. Chris knew Steve would tell his wife all in due course. When the time was right he'd warn her about loose talk causing them problems.

Before they carried on with their leisurely day by the sea, Chris took the opportunity to have private words with Steve. "What's nappening with Barry Montgomery and his friends?"

"The police have thrown the book a them. What with the drugs, a stolen gun, kidnapping and a lot of other crimes we know nothing about, they are safely locked up in Norwich jail awaiting trial."

"Good. They deserve it." Chris nodded vigorously and slapped his mate on the back, then he abruptly changed the subject "Don't think I'm criticizing you, Steve, but you must learn to restore antiques or you'll never make a good living at dealing in them. You can never know too much. With that in mind, I've been thinking."

Steve listened to his mate with interest.

He continued. "If you can come over to my place some weekends, I can put you and Dawn up in my spare room. I can teach you some of the tricks of the trade. Restoration is fifty percent knowhow and fifty percent hard graft. If you can pick up some stock like that lacquered clock you sold me, I will teach you to restore it for sale."

Steve grinned appreciatively. "That would be marvellous. I have also been thinking. That £25,000 will help me out for now but it won't last forever. I have to get better at antique dealing or give it up altogether. I haven't a clue what else I would do, so I've little choice but to get better at it."

Chris was glad his friend saw it that way. "Right. You now know the answer. I'll help teach you."

After their visit to Cley, Chris and Tania drove on to Cromer to have lunch, then they worked their way leisurely back along the North Norfolk coast calling at all the small villages that bordered the sea. After they had tea at Hunstanton they set out for Rutland and home.

It had been a harrowing time since he'd found that hoard of diamonds but things did seem to be on an even keel at last. Chris glanced over at Tania as he drove through Holbeach. She was a nice girl and seemed happy enough in his company. It was a pity that Sara had become so possessive, but it was probably for the best.

I have enjoyed sharing my knowledge and love of antiques with you and hope you have enjoyed the stories woven around them.

This book is the second I have written about Chris Doughty and his life in Barrowick. The first book, - The Dealer and the Devil - An occult thriller - ISBN 9781902474267 - was published in 2012 and is still in print.

In that story I introduced many of the characters met in this book. Hopefully I will continue to draw on my experiences to bring my readers more insights into the fascinating antiques business and the unique county of Rutland, where I now live.

*Rex Merchant*

**Other Fiction by this Author**
**The Runford Chronicles.**
(Adult fantasy novels)
The Faerie Stone  9781902474012

The Tomatoes of Time  9781902474007

The Pied Punch & Judy Man  9781902474069

The Archdruid of Macclesfield  9781902474090

Oswald Gotobed & the Cambeach Ghost  9781902474199

**Historical Novels**
St. Anthony's Piglet  9781902474175

Deeping Fen  9781902474243

**Non-Fiction Books by this Author**
The Spalding Bird Museum  9781902474236

Animal Taxidermy 9781902474137

Bird Taxidermy  9781902474144

Fish Taxidermy  9781902474151

Taxidermy Trophies  9781902474168

Traditional Taxidermy (The above four books in one volume)
9781902474212
Care of the Longcase Clock 9781902474182

Self-Publishing Books  9781902474250